Dawn of the Shadowcasters

The Stevie Vegas Chronicles

Dawn of the Shadowcasters

The Stevie Vegas Chronicles

M. R. Weston

LODESTONE
BOOKS

Winchester, UK
Washington, USA

First published by Lodestone Books, 2014
Lodestone Books is an imprint of John Hunt Publishing Ltd., Laurel House, Station Approach,
Alresford, Hants, SO24 9JH, UK
office1@jhpbooks.net
www.johnhuntpublishing.com

For distributor details and how to order please visit the 'Ordering' section on our website.

A CIP catalogue record for this book is available from the British Library.

Design: Stuart Davies

Printed in the USA by Edwards Brothers Malloy

We operate a distinctive and ethical publishing philosophy in all
areas of our business, from our global network of authors to
production and worldwide distribution.

This book is dedicated to all the caring people in the world – you know who you are. You bring light where there is darkness. You are very special.

Prologue

I met him today. Stevie Vegas. I was always meant to meet him. Part of the plan – that's why I was saved – the daughter of a Shadowcaster, no less.

I am different now to what I was then when my own people turned against me, tried to kill me. Yes, I was born to a Shadowcaster, but I am NOT one of them. I fought against the darkness that engulfed me, tempted me and tried to seduce me. There was a light, far off in my distant self. I clung to that. That and the birth right of my mother who was descended from the Illuminators. The light ran strong in her blood, until they killed her one random but predetermined night – a house invasion the police said…

He skates, Stevie Vegas. He is different from the other boys. The light is very strong in him.

Thank you, oh thank you, Aunt Bessie, for saving me from the Shadowcasters. It wasn't easy to stay out of their vision, but thanks to you I nearly managed it. Stevie Vegas is lucky to have you as an aunt; I have no one, but you're near enough, Aunt, to me.

Aside from my horrid birth right, my struggle to escape the Shadowcasters and hiding desperately from their view, I try to be like any normal teenage girl. Sound stupid? Well, what's normal I say?

I have pretty hair, I know that. It's soft and shiny, the color of dawn. And my eyes are pretty too; the darkest of brown. Intense, yes – they sometimes make people uncomfortable but that's just because they know what I see. I see them.

And I ride as fast as the wind – not a skateboard like Stevie Vegas – no, I prefer the raw power of a motocross bike and the idea that it's not supposed to be a 'girl thing.' But I'm no ordinary girl any more than Stevie Vegas is a normal boy. We are both

Shadowcaster and Illuminator alike.

But these days, with the help of Aunt Bessie and those that follow the light, I am just as much Illuminator as them, and the plan is for me to help Stevie Vegas succeed. He will need my help; there is no surer thing.

They're coming for him. I can hear them from behind the veil that separates the real world and its underbelly. Like weeds they'll try and break to the surface, into the shadows. Some of them are here, like me, in Valley Dale. Ordinary people, doing ordinary things. To look at them, you would never guess, but they are here nevertheless. Their dark auras surround them like the black night envelops the quarter moon.

We Illuminators are here too. Opposite sides of the coin and before it's over we'll see what chance has in store for all of us.

Stevie Vegas has no idea who I am, but when the time is right I will tell him that his Aunt Bessie saw good in me – saw the light within the darkness. Nothing is ever simple, is it? Nor ever that black and white? Shades of grey are everywhere, but what counts are the choices we make. I choose to be an Illuminator and I choose to fight with every breath in my body against what is coming.

Stevie Vegas will have many friends when they come for him. He will need them. I am one of them.

I can hear the far off voices of the Shadowcasters, whispering on the wind. I am old before my time. I should not know what I do, hear what I do, and see what I do.

Why can't I have the same uncomplicated life any 13-year-old teenager has. They like nothing better than to lip sync to their favorite singer's songs, or spend hours straightening their hair, painting nails purple, shopping for clothes – parents catering to every whim.

Nah, that's not me. My Yamaha 250 is my family. And Aunt Bessie too, and because of her, Stevie Vegas.

It's time for a ride now, out beyond Valley Dale's limits where the woods begin and, if you look hard enough, the hundreds of trails that lead down to the river, and onto the sea.

Life is not all threatening darkness, thank God. I can smell the not so far off ocean. I can feel the sun on my arms. I see the blueness of the sky and the mighty oak that lives outside my window. I know somewhere Stevie Vegas is practicing his skateboard stunts, just like I am about to ride to the ocean.

For the moment, we can be like other teenagers. The darkness will come, soon enough.

Chapter One

Nightmares Revisited

Stevie Vegas stirred fitfully in his dreams. Dark shadows penetrated the safe fabric of the reality of his new life in Valley Dale, just as certainly as Jacob Barron sent his thoughts across the landscape from where he lay in a coma, at Smithson.

He tossed. Snippets of that day were making their way back to him through this night of dreams – the stranger's hooded face who had moved in just that day, next door. Stevie had bumped into him by chance as the hooded man was directing the moving truck into his driveway.

While Stevie was spent from a hard session at the skatepark practicing his big air twists, he couldn't help feel the odd sensation of immediate dislike of the stranger. He thought about the Shadowcasters, briefly, for the first time in a year. No, not in Valley Dale, he reasoned. Smithson and the Barrons were far away, like a long forgotten nightmare, and life had returned to normal since those dark days when he first learned he was an Illuminator and battled the Shadowcasters.

Throughout that following year after Smithson, Stevie had buried the past, concentrated on his schoolwork, reveled in his family life, and placed the Illuminator stone far away in the back of his sock drawer. He neither used his powers of Extra Sensory Perception, nor made things happen with the strength of his mind. He buried his Illuminator powers underneath layers of denial. There were times, and battles, he wanted to forget. Like all 13-year-old boys, he was preoccupied with growing up and despite the scars of Smithson, and the threat that one day the Shadowcasters would turn up, his thoughts easily turned to the simple pleasures of living. Dark thoughts were banished, his brother Jem had fully recovered from his accident at the hands of the Shadowcasters, and Stevie had slept peacefully at night. That was until now.

His nemesis Chris Barron's face appeared in quick succession to the hooded man's veiled, piercing eyes. He recalled Chris Barron's parting warning to him as his family were leaving Smithson, "Sleep while you can, young Illuminator, there will be a reckoning for you. Not today, but someday, soon. That day will dawn when you least expect it, when you experience the world as better place, and you will learn that the Shadowcasters' influence can never be put down. And while you will never know when and how, your day of reckoning will come."

Stevie had spat on the ground in front of Chris Barron – something he never did, and especially to an adult – the 'leading light' of Smithson no less, and turned away, propelling his skate-board slowly down the road while pushing his thoughts out toward him. "I am not afraid. I do not cling to the cliff's edge waiting for fear to make decisions for me. I stand strong against you and all the others like you. I am an Illuminator."

When his family had left Smithson so quickly after Stevie and his Aunt Bessie's desperate midnight dash to spirit the cursed stones away from the Barron estate and drown them in the depths of the Katounga River, they had settled into Valley Dale, and Stevie felt happy. But his happiness was always marked by a back of the mind worry no 13-year-old should feel.

He had reasoned it away with time. The cursed stones, the source of Chris Barron's power, were gone but there had been one stone they could not recover, that of Chris Barron's son, Jacob. But, again, he had reasoned away that Jacob Barron was laid up in a hospital bed of his own making. He had fallen during the skateboarding duel with Stevie, when evil incantations had backfired, like karma having the last laugh.

Jacob Barron had been rushed to Smithson Emergency and had slipped into a coma, which he had not, to this day, recovered from. Stevie had struggled with remorse and, even in Valley

Dale, felt the cold weight of guilt, which was present more often than he cared to admit.

In his dreams that night he heard Jacob's voice too against the wind outside on that dark night, rattling the panes, and disturbing the peace of the Vegas household. Like that day in the Valley Dale schoolyard when the wind was blowing the leaves in circles outside the classroom window whispering its hidden messages, Jacob Barron was talking with someone from behind a shroud-like veil. "It is going to plan, we are growing stronger again. They are gathering. With your help, we will triumph. No light will penetrate the blackness of our being…"

Stevie sat bolt upright in bed and reached frantically for his night lamp. Fumbling with the switch, breath sucked inwards, he finally found the light, which flooded his room, driving back the darkness. He was sweating, and dazed. He looked around and found the one thing of comfort – his skateboard. He shook his head in disbelief. Why, why was he dreaming about the hooded man and about Jacob Barron? He looked skyward with what seemed like a pathetic plea. *Please God, not again. Not here and in Valley Dale.*

His thoughts turned to anger. He did not want to fight battles any more. It had nearly cost his brother's life, turned his family upside down, and inside out, as they had spent the better part of a year back in Valley Dale building up their veterinary practice again. Jem had not been the same since his accident that fateful day when the Shadowcasters drove him toward an impossible climb, always honing in on the weakest link. Well his brother was not the weakest link in the Vegas family. Stevie gritted his teeth. He didn't know why, but his resolve rallied against the thought that he might meet with the Barrons again – he was not afraid.

He hadn't used his Extra Sensory Perception in a long while, but in the middle of the night, sitting upright in his childhood bed, he thought of his Aunt Bessie who was the other Illuminator in the Vegas family. "Aunt Bessie," he whispered into the night.

"It's starting again."

He got up and quickly went to his chest of drawers. Opening the top one where his socks and baseball caps were, he reached into the furthest of corners. He felt the warmth pulsating from the back of the drawer even before his fingers reached his Illuminator stone. He picked up the necklace and relief flooded through him. Somehow, in that split instance, everything was all right again. He hadn't worn that necklace in a year, but now he slipped it over his head. The blackness of his nightmares receded, just like the dark ocean of his fear. Yes, he was full of anxiety about what he knew was coming – but not afraid. Never afraid.

Stevie let sleep take him then, one hand on his Illuminator stone and the other resting on his skateboard which he had stood beside his bed.

Morning dawned just like any other and he heard his mother's urgent tones from downstairs. "Stevie, Stevie Vegas, will you get up and start getting ready. You will be late otherwise and I have a little dog that's just been brought in with a broken leg. I need to go into surgery in twenty minutes and I won't be able to drop you at school."

Stevie jumped out of bed at his mother's voice. She very rarely raised it, and he knew that there was a veterinarian emergency on her hands. He would have to take Jem to school, but at least he could skate the mile or so to Valley Dale Elementary, while Jem rode his BMX. Ah, yes, there was that guardrail on the stairs leading down into Fontenoy Street. It was one of his favorite places to Grind. Perhaps he could practice that kickflip off the rail, though it was pretty high and his landing may not be smooth…

As he ran past Jem's door he noticed him on the computer. "Hey, bro, ace it up, what are you playing, you know that Mum and Dad say no gaming before school."

Jem dragged his gaze away from the computer. "Shut up,

Stevie, you're not the only one who's good at stuff. I've just reached a new level on this new game, and it takes strategy to do that. It's not just about shooting 'em up, you know."

"Whatever, bro, but you better put your skates on, 'cause Mum is cracking the whip something bad." His brother grimaced at him.

"I'm not the champion skater in this family. You are, remember? Leave me alone and stop always trying to run my life. I'm not you."

Stevie shot a puzzled look at his brother. "Sorry, Jem," he muttered on his way to the bathroom, under his breath. "I only do things 'cause I care. Sorreee!"

Both he and Jem were soon downstairs, enjoying the bacon and egg breakfast their mother had cooked earlier that morning.

"Stevie, how many times do I have to tell you? Do not bring your skateboard to the table," his mum pleaded. "It doesn't have to lean on the table next to your chair. It will be all right in the lounge. Now, go and put it there and don't bring it to the table again."

He did as he was told, but not before he winked at his dad.

"Oh, come on, Syl, it won't hurt, you know." His dad was always ready to come to the defense of his son's hobbies. He was less tough on his two boys than Sylvia Vegas, though goodness knows teenage boys needed a few boundaries. Mrs. Vegas supplied them but Stevie knew, like Jem and his dad, that he would not bring his skateboard to the table again...well, at least for one week.

It was a quick breakfast for the Vegas family that morning. His mum worked in the annex at the side of the house, which doubled as their vet surgery given they had to let the rented practice go as a result of the upheaval in moving to Smithson, and then back to Valley Dale. Money was a little tight when they had returned, so the double garage had been converted into vet rooms to save money. His dad, on the other hand, was doing house calls to the ritzy part of town – not something he overly enjoyed as he specialized in larger animals, but it did bring the extra money in when doting, rich pet owners wanted their dog's nails clipped.

"Well, Vegas boys," his father said brightly getting up from the table. "I'm off to Green Valley to tend to a spoilt pooch."

"And I'm off to do some real work," his mother said, giving her husband a kiss on the cheek. "You boys finish your breakfast quickly, and out that door please within two minutes. I'm just next door you know, and I can hear the front door slam."

Stevie smiled at Jem. "Coming, Jemmy?" He waited for his brother's sarcasm, but, surprisingly it didn't come.

Jem spooned the last of his eggs into his mouth and gave Stevie a tired look that said, 'It's OK' and the harsh words of that morning were forgotten.

They were just about out the door, when his mother called to him.

"Oh, Stevie, Aunt Bessie rang this morning. She wants you to call her back tonight. She's travelling at the moment, but said she wanted to catch up with you. Everything all right?" Mrs. Vegas asked, a slight worry underscoring the faint lines on her forehead.

Stevie too was puzzled, but then remembered his nightmare. "Yeah, Mum…err everything is OK, I just wanted to say hello to Aunt Bessie and make sure she's not overdoing things, you know travelling around the country…"

"Umm, OK, then," his mother called. "Now off to school and easy on the skating tricks on your way."

And with that, the Vegas family began their seemingly normal day. Only Stevie was preoccupied, remembering his dark, nighttime dreams.

Chapter Two

Normal Teenage Stuff

Stevie chose to skate home from school that day, while Jem went to soccer practice. His adventurous spirit made sure he took a route home that was new. Parkour on a skateboard was his thing at the moment. It allowed him to jump off any ledge in sight, Grind any metal rail he came across, and practice his Ollies, Kickflips and Twists at any strategic point of the journey. But the street he came to was odd and strangely familiar, as though he had somehow been there before, and certainly there was no concrete or metal – two of his favorite skateboarding spring-boards. No, this street was old, and definitely unfamiliar.

Elm Street the sign said and, true to its name, a sinister avenue of old Elms stood guard over its residents. Stevie shivered slightly, kicked up his skateboard and walked down the street on foot. He was intrigued by this new vista, and somehow felt he should be there – as if it was the right time, and right place for him to be.

Huge, dark looking, weatherboard mansions characterized the street, but there was nothing glorious or grand about them – they looked like they'd been there for centuries. Stevie was sure they housed half-dead, zombie characters that would make their appearance to him any minute…any minute now.

He was thinking he had had enough of the crumbly, broken-down and eerie street, when the front door of a grey-ish green home opened. He let his attention stay on the girl who emerged. Her golden hair was a giveaway. It was that new girl he had met in class…Mary Lou.

"Nova," she said, walking quickly up to him and extending her hand. "You're Stevie Vegas. We met the other day at school. Nice skateboard."

He gave her an extremely puzzled look. "How did you...never mind, yes I'm Stevie. What are you doing here? I mean in this crabby old street. I would have thought only old people live here."

She shot him a charming smile, which transformed her dark and intense eyes into warm, friendly beacons, which said, 'See, I'm not so bad after all.'

"I live here, silly, with my father – he's the new vet in town, just started up his practice and so we've come to live here."

Stevie surveyed her, instantly put out that her dad may be in some way responsible for the downturn in his parents fortunes. Of course, that was not true. He knew that, but he was wary of her nevertheless...though on this sunny afternoon in Valley Dale, instead of disliking this strange girl, he was drawn to her.

Out of habit, he tried to read her thoughts, but met with a blank.

As if she was reading his thoughts, she said, "Hey, I'm sorry...is something wrong?"

She was dressed in jeans and a black T-shirt, which read, 'Riders Rock,' and had a picture of a Harley Davidson emblazoned down the front.

"Err...no, I was just looking at your T-shirt. You don't by chance ride a Harley, do you?"

She laughed then and her face opened up like an early morning flower to the sun. Stevie could now see just how pretty Mary Lou Nova was when the weight of life was not bearing down on her.

"No way, silly. I'm too young to be riding a Harley and they're way too expensive for me, but I do have a 250 Yammy out the back. You ride?"

Now it was Stevie's turn to laugh. He held his skateboard up, showing her the slogan on the bottom, 'ramp, air, wind, sky, fly.' "I'm more into non-motorized sports, where you have to rely on yourself for the thrills."

"Humph," she snorted, in deep disgust. "Don't tell me there is no skill in motocross riding. In fact, if you don't get it right on some of the trails round here, you can kiss your…" she patted her behind, "…goodbye."

Stevie laughed again. A deep laugh that relaxed him totally in this strange girl's company.

"You are funny, Mary Lou Nova. I can say I've never met anyone quite like you, and riding motocross on a 250 Yammy. Impressive."

The front door of her house swung open for the second time that day. Mr. Nova called to his daughter.

"Mary Lou, it's time for supper. Inside, please."

Instantly, he felt a sense of gloom descend upon them, and guilt too, as if they had been caught in a conspiracy.

As if they had, Mary Lou lowered her tone.

"I've got to go now, Vegas, you shouldn't be here. But we'll meet again at school, and one afternoon soon, I'll take you for a ride in the woods. That's if you're game."

"Sure," he said, as she rushed away, as if the devil himself had called her. "Anytime. I'm game."

She was gone then, and Stevie stared at the odd, eerie looking house again. Elm Street was not a friendly place he decided. He put his board down and skated off as quickly as his foot could propel him.

What a strange afternoon, he was thinking, when he remembered he would be late for taekwondo lessons with Jem. It was something his mum and dad had insisted on when they returned from Smithson, as a way of learning self-defense just in case the boys got into trouble again, but to this day they didn't know that the Shadowcasters were behind their troubles in Smithson, and Stevie was not going to tell them if he didn't have to. They were safer if they didn't know, Stevie reasoned.

Safe against the Shadowcasters, Stevie thought wryly, as he skated into Sun Lee's gym, knowing there was no martial art discipline on this earth that would protect against the power of the cursed stones and the dark thought power of the Shadowcasters. Jem was waiting impatiently out the front.

"Stevie, where you been?" he said, frantically picking up his gear from the sidewalk. "You know our lesson begins at 4.30 pm – it has done for the last two months, or did you forget?"

Stevie made for the front door. "No I didn't, I was…talking to a friend."

Jem gave him a look of disgust as they entered Sun Lee's. It wasn't the newest gym in Valley Dale. In fact, it was rather old looking compared to the lycra clad, expensively laid out gyms in the newer part of town. No tall yuppy men with perfect abs worked out here. Instead, you could smell the scent of sesame seeds and fish sauce, and the pungent but familiar aroma of garlic and ginger coming from the Lee's kitchen out the back. This gym was also the home to the Lees, who, Stevie had found out the other day, were distant relatives of Tom Lee, his one friend against the Smithson Shadowcasters. That one fact had made him consent, rather than say no to his mother's insistence they learn self-defense. Any relative of Tom's had to be worth meeting, he thought.

It was dark inside the gym, with its three roped rings, boxing bags hanging from its rafters and general gym equipment in the corner. Mr. Lee insisted they pulled weights and use the exercise bikes to increase their general fitness after a taekwondo lesson.

Stevie and Jem looked around for Mr. Lee's familiar face, but instead saw a young man, no more than about 18 years old, coming toward them.

"Hey, you fellas, you must be the Vegas boys?" They nodded, slightly bewildered by the stranger's youth. He was stockily built, with muscled arms and legs. His longish black hair fell over friendly, welcoming brown eyes.

Jem broke the silence. "Yeah, that's us. Who are you?"

"Sun Lee is my grandfather. He's had to leave town for a

couple of days, and I'll be taking you for this afternoon's lesson. My name is Bren Lee."

"You? You're not much older than us," Jem said.

"Ssshhh, Jem," Stevie said, digging his brother in the ribs. He glanced at the stranger, sizing him up.

Intuitively, Stevie knew the boy possessed strength of body, and mind. He noted the dragon tattoo on the boy's arm, the gold cross round the boy's neck and his confident swagger. This was a young man not to be pushed around. He just knew that, despite the boy's friendly demeanor.

Stevie extended his hand. "I'm Stevie," he said, looking Bren Lee straight in the eyes.

Bren Lee stared back, for an instant, before he relaxed, a slight grin creasing the sides of his mouth.

"And this," Stevie said, "is my bro, Jem."

"I don't need any introductions from you, Stevie. I can do that myself."

Stevie made a face at Bren Lee, who continued to nod and smile at the Vegas boys.

"So," Jem said. "You taking us for today's lesson? We betta get started, 'cause I've got stuff to do at home."

Stevie grinned and pushed the invisible boundary with his brother. "Yeah, computer games for four hours straight. He's a shadow walker, you see."

Jem's face blushed a bright red. "Shut up, Stevie, I'm sick of you. Always making fun of me. There's no difference in hours on the computer getting to the next level of a game millions play, than the hours you spend on your stupid skateboard. Yeah, skateboarders are just stupid – all of 'em."

Bren Lee clapped his hand once and then brought them into a perfect diamond shape, closing his eyes. "It does you two no good to be separate, to compete with one another. Brothers should respect each another like the river respects the stone it flows over. River, water and stone are of the same thing."

Jem looked away with scorn. "Zen freak," he muttered to himself, and Stevie hurried to the change rooms, motioning to an irritable Jem to get his doobuk robes on for training. Once in the ring, Bren Lee indicated they would be practicing blocks.

"Blocks defend you against attacks, from punches and kicks to the head and the body," Bren Lee said, adopting the Apkubi Seogi stance. Oh, and by the way, your stance is everything. It's the foundation from the ground up, and will make the difference when someone catches you off guard. Anchor yourself, Vegas brothers, for you never know who is more than willing to try and push you off your feet."

Stevie and Jem both adopted the Apkubi Seogi stance and waited for Bren Lee's next move. This, Stevie Vegas thought, was shaping up to be a good lesson.

Bren Lee continued, "Blocks must be fast, strong and timing is everything…and use two arms. Most people favor one, but it makes them weak. Use what you have, your two arms, and you will be in balance, not one side more powerful than the other to compensate for a weakness – two arms and hands, blocking like this."

He demonstrated the blocking techniques while Stevie and Jem looked on, awestruck by his skill. Then it was their turn to practice what they'd learned.

Low blocks, middle blocks, high blocks – Bren Lee put the two boys through their paces for the next 40 minutes, until Stevie was the one to yield. "Is that it, I'm due at the skatepark for a quick session before dinner."

Bren Lee looked up, as if surprised by Stevie's request. He gazed at Stevie for a few moments before answering. "Yes, young Vegas, it's time to end our lessons…only I would say to you that skateboarding is not so different from martial arts. Anchor, block, and attack. Think about it."

Stevie smiled. "You are right, Bren Lee. That's good advice. When I skate I must stay strong on my board – balance is everything, and I must concentrate on my own tricks, not someone trying to outdo me. And finally, I must execute the trick of tricks that puts my competitor off guard – yes, anchor, block, attack, or maybe anchor, attack and block."

Bren Lee laughed. "You Stevie Vegas are one of a kind."

Jem piped up in between the camaraderie. "Well if it's OK with my skateboarding brother who's a legend in his own mind, and Bren sensi person, can I go? I've got a battle to fight on my new computer game."

Stevie shook his head, smiling at Bren Lee. "My brother is, well, preoccupied with computers at the moment."

Stevie and Jem changed back into their jeans and T-shirts.

"Come on, Stevie," Jem said, impatient to get home.

"Righto," Stevie answered, hurrying to catch Jem who was just about out the door. If he had time, he could get a bit of skateboarding in before dark.

Only Bren Lee's thoughts were still on the lesson. The Vegas boys would need a lot more teaching before they were through, he thought, none the least in how to be brothers.

Chapter 3

Signs in the Wind

The sun shone, the sky was blue and Stevie Vegas was getting some big air at Valley Dale's skate park. As he dropped in, he couldn't think of anything else but his next trick, a McGill McTwist. Gaining momentum, he felt the familiar rush of air as he executed the perfect move. He finished off with a few grinds and Ollies before skating off the ramp. He had 15 minutes to get to school, and he didn't want to be late, again. There would be hell to pay at home if his teacher sent the third note home this term.

He wiped the sweat from his forehead, tucked his skateboard under his arm and went to retrieve his backpack from the nearby seats. Valley Dale's skatepark wasn't great, a bit small for his liking, but he knew every inch of it, every grind rail, every ramp, incline and decline. Most of all, it was home, and he always performed well against its challenges. Out of the corner of his eye, he noticed a young girl sitting nearby, under a shady tree. It was the girl he kept bumping into – Mary Lou Nova.

He was half-inclined to give her a miss and skate to school, so as not to be late, but something compelled him to venture over and simply say, "Hi."

"That McTwist was pretty awesome," she said, shading her eyes from the sun with a textbook. "Just catching up on some study. And, you know, it's quiet here."

"Yeah, I know. It's good, 'specially when things are intense at home," he replied.

She smiled that nice smile again which made her eyes crinkle in the corner. When she smiled, he thought, she looked like any other 13-year-old girl, but when she didn't...well she looked like she had 'seen' some things she wasn't supposed to.

"You know we're gonna be late if we don't pull some Gs."

It was his turn to smile. "Pull some Gs. What the hell does that mean?"

"You know, get a move on. Put your skates on. Whatever," she said, getting up and slinging her backpack over her shoulder. "Want to walk and talk?"

He gave her a look, which said, 'OK you lead the way,' and they began to walk in the direction of school. It was only a few blocks and if they walked quickly they'd make the first bell.

Stevie gazed across the park, deep in thought. He had argued, again, with Jem that morning. He really didn't know what had got into him these days. And his mum was cranky with his dad. His dad on the other hand, just shut up and took it with that ever-present look of resignation that he wore now. These days, money was tight in the Vegas household. With two new vet practices opening up in town within the last few months, and Jem withdrawing to his room every spare moment, he was starting to wonder what was happening to his family.

It was as if a dark cloud had descended on them, like a hangover from Smithson, only there were no Barrons or Shadowcasters in sight this time. Even at 13, he knew you had to take the good with the bad in life and that, sometimes, life had its challenges, but this was different. It seemed over the past few months, everything had gone wrong for them. First it was his parents' work, which seemed to dry up overnight, and then Jem had begun to change – one minute he was a normal 12-year-old, the next he was street smart and cynical, and cold all at the same time. Stevie had begun to think he didn't know Jem at all and that was out of the ordinary because in the past they had been as close as two brothers could be, or so he thought.

The mysterious stranger had moved in next door and, it appeared to him, was everyone's friend in the street, except the Vegas family's. He knew they were being excluded from street barbecues and often he would catch the hooded man in a conversation with a neighbor, only to stop talking when he walked past. At school, a couple of new teachers had started this term and were continually on his case. His skateboarding mentor had got a new job in another state and, bang, there went Stevie's skating teacher and buddy. What had he done to make the world such a horrible place, all of a sudden?

He had spoken to his Aunt Bessie last night and, as usual, there was no fooling her. She had asked him question after question, about the new people who had moved into Valley Dale – teachers, neighbors and new vets. And then she had asked him if he was dreaming. At first he misunderstood her, and had replied quite strongly that he felt there was a dark cloud over his family.

"No, dreaming…any nightmares?" she had insisted.

"Oh, yeah…a few." He really didn't want to talk about it, because he still felt guilty over Jacob Barron's accident, and guilt has a way of eroding good sense, and peace of mind. Pretty soon if you dwell on it, it leads to fear and Stevie was not fearful by nature. No, he reasoned the best way to deal with things was not to talk about them.

"Stevie, you've got to talk to me about the things that are worrying you," his Aunt Bessie had replied.

"When has talking ever solved anything, Aunt Bessie?" He was stubborn when he wanted to be.

But his aunt had kept probing, like most adults do when they know they are not getting the full story.

"Have you been reading anyone's thoughts lately, or 'seeing' auras? Have you been using your Illuminator powers?" she continued.

His voice held only a slight edge compared to the anger that was welling up in him. "No, Aunt Bessie, I haven't. And I don't want to. Illuminator *powers* led to trouble for our family. The best thing we can do is forget that Smithson ever happened."

She was silent for a moment. "You know Stevie you can't deny who you are."

He had wanted to finish the conversation then. Far better to go and watch the latest cartoon on TV, there was no danger in that.

"Aunt Bessie, I don't mean to be cranky with you, but sometimes things are best left alone."

She sighed. "If I wasn't travelling on important business, I'd come down to Valley Dale and tell you that ignoring trouble will not necessarily make it go away. But you know that don't you, Stevie? I'll try and get down within the next few months, and I just want you to know that I'm trying to get to the bottom of things where I am for you. As always, I'm your biggest fan, young man."

He didn't want her to worry. "It's OK, Aunt Bessie. It's just these dreams, well nightmares. They're happening every night for the past few weeks…"

"Stevie you need to wear your Illuminator necklace. Don't hide it in the sock drawer…yes I know that's what you do. Wear it, and the dreams will get better…well at least you will have more control over them."

He promised to do that and very nearly asked her to drop what she was doing and come to Valley Dale. At the very least, it would make his mum happy as Aunt Bessie was her favorite and had practically raised her. But he didn't, saying his goodbyes instead and telling her to look after herself, wherever and whatever she was doing on her travels.

His thoughts were interrupted by his companion. "Stevie, Stevie Vegas, are you listening to me?"

He had been so deep in thought he hadn't noticed she had been talking at him for minutes.

"I'm sorry," he said, glancing at her surprised face. "I was somewhere else…a lot on my mind."

"I can see THAT." She laughed. They walked in silence, for a moment. He was conscious that he hardly knew this girl he was with.

"Umm…when I first met you at school, I remember you saying you knew my Aunt Bessie. How well do you know her?" he said.

She looked at him sharply. "You don't know, do you?"

"Know what? I'm not a mind reader you know." He couldn't help smile to himself when he said that. "What am I'm supposed to know?"

"That your Aunt Bessie saved my life when I was a very young girl and we have been friends ever since. She's told me about you…even asked me to keep an eye on you."

Stevie threw back his head and laughed hard. That was the funniest thing he'd heard all morning. "You, keep an eye on me. I don't think so. It would be me keeping an eye on you."

"Well, OK then, if that's the way you want it…" she said, over her shoulder as she began to jog off. "I'll race you the rest of the way to school, and no skateboarding right. Just you, me and four legs."

It was a playful challenge and there was no doubting she could run…run like the wind actually. She had been spot on when she said they'd have to pull some Gs to get to school.

He laughed to himself for the second time that morning. She would probably beat him; she was so quick legged, but that didn't matter. His thoughts were temporarily off his worries and onto everyday things – even if he was getting beaten by a girl.

They arrived at the school in time for the first bell. Teenagers were everywhere and the schoolyard was crowded, as they tried to make their way to class.

"You know, Mary Lou, you're not half bad. You can run and you're not too boring."

She gave him a playful punch in the arm. "Hey, you don't know the half of it. If you think I'm fast on two legs you should see me on four cylinders."

He laughed again, and knew straight away he was making a firm friend in this girl, and it struck him it was the first real girl *friend* he'd ever had.

She gave him that nice smile again, as though she was reading his thoughts. For the briefest moment, he opened his mind to her despite, himself. And he felt her happiness and the thought that she was thinking that he was one of the nicest boys she'd met.

"We have a lot in common, you know?" he said to her, smiling before he even said it, knowing that she couldn't possibly know he was reading her mind.

She smiled back. "Oh, I think we have more in common than you think."

Stevie gave her a puzzled look, momentarily, and was on the verge of asking what she meant, when his thoughts began to blur. It felt like he was being punched in the chest. He sucked in his breath and looked questioningly at Mary Lou, but she returned his look with concern and just a hint of…fear. He instinctively turned toward the direction of where the dark energy was coming. It came in waves at him, pulsating through the air; each pulse had the effect of a small stun gun on him. He was really struggling for breath. His hand went instinctively to his necklace and he felt a momentary easing of the dark energy that threatened to engulf him. Ahead, about 10 yards, was a boy, about the same age as him. Stevie only noticed the blackest of auras before he passed out, and slid to the ground at Mary Lou's feet.

When he came to, the school principal Mr. Everett Dewbury was standing over him.

"Stevie, Stevie Vegas – are you all right, son. You've passed out. What seems to have happened here?"

Stevie began to get to his feet with Mary Lou's help, stronger now the boy had disappeared.

"Ah, sir…I'm not really sure. Umm, I've been skating this morning and the sun's pretty hot," he said.

The Principal shook his head. He had known Stevie since first grade and he liked the boy.

"Stevie, I understand your love of skateboarding but this is a school day. Can I suggest you leave the aerials until the weekend? Now let's get you off to sickbay. I want nurse to check you over before we send you off to class. Mary Lou, there's no need for you to be late for class too. Off you go."

He put a supportive arm under Stevie's arm and motioned him in the direction of the teacher's staffroom, where sickbay was located. Stevie had just enough time to give Mary Lou a quick look, which said he was surprised, and puzzled, by what had just occurred. She returned his gaze with an equal amount of…disbelief and concern, as if she had fewer answers than he had.

Principal Dewbury was quite oblivious to what had just occurred – how could he know what Stevie had just experienced. Stevie, on the other hand, was deep in thought and not really listening to the Principal's calm, steady, voice beside him. No, his mind was churning. Without a doubt he knew he had just confronted…a Shadowcaster. It had to be, no one else would have been able to throw him off balance so easily. But who? And why? And in Valley Dale. His thoughts were jumbled and he knew he needed to think this through calmly. The residual effects of the attack were still with him.

"Well, Stevie, you appear recovered but I'm not going to take any chances. You can spend the first period with nurse until we're sure that you are OK," Principal Dewbury said.

They entered the clinic and the Principal directed him to one of the three beds that were freshly made up. "Now, rest please, while I go and get Nurse Matheson."

Stevie sat on the side of the bed. He had recovered his sense of balance, physically, but there were questions that needed urgent answers swirling through his confused mind. Alone, and in the quiet of the clinic, he did what he hadn't done in these many long months since Smithson. He sent out a deliberate thought to the only person he knew would have the answers.

With all his being, he sent out an urgent plea for help to his Aunt Bessie. He imagined her face and looked into her eyes with his thoughts and mouthed the words silently, pushing them out into he knew not what. Thin air? But it was all he had in that moment. "Aunt Bessie, it's happening again. Please come, please come, please come…"

Chapter Four

Jem's New Friend

The skies above Valley Dale were black with the threatening storm. Although it was the middle of summer, these occasional squalls blew in from the nearby ocean, lasting briefly throughout a mid-afternoon, and raining down a deluge before subsiding, only to reveal sunshine in all its sparkling glory. But for now, blue sky crackled with the looming thunder, the air chilled and the dark clouds gathered.

Jem Vegas was making his way slowly back from school. He kicked at the stones and tufts of grass as he walked, and his mood was as dark as the overhead sky. He had seen Stevie today with his new *girlfriend* – that strange girl with the straw-colored hair and piercing black eyes from Elm Street. Oh, he knew all about Elm Street. He had been delivering newspapers there one Saturday morning and had noticed her sitting by her window. She had given him the strangest look…before her father came striding down their front path to introduce himself. Said he was the new vet in town and he knew who Jem was, the son of a fellow veterinarian. He also said he knew all about Jem's talent on the soccer field, and on the cricket pitch. It was nice for a change to be recognized as someone other than Stevie Vegas' brother. Very nice indeed.

Mr. Nova had also suggested that if he wanted to make a bit of extra pocket money, he could mow their lawn and do some odd jobs round the place. He liked the strange girl's father, even if he didn't like that girl much.

As he turned into suburban Hill Street, he could see his home up in the distance. Stevie was out the front skating on the road, which was relatively free from traffic at this time of the day. He could see his brother execute his grinds on the curb. Typical with

Stevie that every waking moment was spent on that damned skateboard. He kicked at the dirt in front of him and slowed his pace. He really didn't want to go home and he didn't really understand why. Ever since Smithson and the bullies, and his fall from the building he was climbing as a dare from them, things had changed. He'd changed. It was like the fall had unleashed something inside. No longer did he want to be the son everyone overlooked. He wanted to be somebody, and most of all, he wanted to be better than his brother.

"Hey," he heard a voice behind him call. "Jem Vegas, isn't it?" It was the new kid who'd arrived at school today.

"Yeah, who wants to know?"

The boy caught up to him and Jem had a chance to look him over. He was roughly the same age as him. Tall and athletic, he thought to himself. Good at sports no doubt and probably a limelighter, like Stevie, or just another bully that saw him as an easy mark. Either way, he quietly resolved to give him slip as soon as he could.

"Eh, ease up there," the boy said, giving Jem a promising smile. "I just wanted to introduce myself. "My name is Devlin Hood. I've moved in next door. My dad's the new general manager on the city council here."

Jem decided that despite the boy's friendliness, he couldn't care less about who he was and why he had decided to be friendly towards him.

"Whatever. Good for you."

The boy was momentarily put off but appeared to want to keep walking with Jem. This annoyed him. He really didn't do much talking to strangers, and these days had no desire to interact with anyone. He'd rather be on his computer and playing Vision Quest which was his latest game at the moment. He'd reached elite status and if he could only crack the last two levels, he would earn the right to be an avatar. Oh, what he would create when he reached that status. His avatar would have the power to beat anybody, the bullies and his brother too. But the boy persisted.

"I like Vision Quest at the moment. I'm an avatar gold status. You know that game? I bet you like gaming. I can tell," the boy said.

Jem stopped in his tracks, still mistrustful and not ready to give up his stubborn decision to limit his contact with everyone at the moment. "Who did you say you were? You said you'd moved in next door to me?"

The boy nodded and smiled again, a little more assuredly. He pulled out an iPod and thrust it into Jem's hands. "Here, my iPod is loaded with the latest stuff. You can borrow it if you like?"

Jem looked sideways at Devlin. "What's the catch?"

"No catch," he replied. "From one gamer to another – you know, the brotherhood and all that. We gotta stick together."

For the first time since their meeting, Jem gave the stranger a full look. He noted the boy's expensive clothes, his brand new street shoes, and the confident expression in the boy's eyes – and it was all directed at him, Jem Vegas.

"Ok then, no catches right?" he said, tucking the iPod into his school bag. "I'll check it out tonight and let you know how I go. You online?"

The boy gave a triumphant smile. "You betcha. Go onto Vision Quest, we can partner if you like?"

Jem's eyes widened. "Really, me partner with you…an avatar gold?"

"As I said, we brothers have gotta stick together and that means equals. If I can help you get want you want, I will. I like you, Jem Vegas, and you're like me. We go after what we want, not what other people want us to do. Understand?"

"Yes, I understand." He thought about telling Devlin that he had been doing what others expected of him all his life…and he was tired of it. He wanted to be his own person, but his real brother was always getting in the way. It was always about Stevie and never about him, and he was getting tired of it. If his mum and dad raved one more time about Stevie's skateboarding, or how good he was with the chores, or how responsible he was…he'd be sick. And then there was that little matter in Smithson. If he hadn't been Stevie's brother he would not have been targeted by Jacob Barron and the bullies. But he kept his thoughts to himself that day. Instead he walked the remaining distance home with Devlin and said his farewells at the front gate, promising to meet up with him that night online.

Jem noticed Stevie had gone inside. Good. He was sure if Stevie met Devlin, Stevie would want to monopolize his newfound friend. He entered the front door quietly, overhearing his mum and dad in the kitchen, arguing again about money. This house, his parents, his brother's stupid nightmares of late…what did any of it really matter? The only thing that was any good in his life at the moment was his success in the online world. Yeah, he was really someone there. So he slipped quietly up to his room and flicked the on switch of his laptop. He smiled as the Vision Quest page came into view.

In the room next door, yards away, Stevie Vegas sat on the edge of his bed, his eyes closed. For the past 30 minutes he'd been struggling with a blackness that threatened to overcome him. Like the turn he'd had at school that morning, he felt as though he was going to pass out. The nightmares he'd been experiencing were revisiting him in his waking thoughts. Inside his head the far off voices began again, whispering voices from behind a dark veil. He tried to block them out. What was happening to him and why wasn't his necklace working this time? He ran his fingers over it, hoping that through his touch it would drive the voices and the blackness away. But it didn't. They came through thick and fast. He lay down and thought hard about what Aunt Bessie would do, and then remembered the protective spell she had caste in Smithson, the night they battled the Shadowcasters and stole the cursed stone. It was a white light that she had placed around the Vegas bungalow. He didn't know how to do that, but he tried. Concentrating all his thoughts on his necklace, he pushed the whiteness of it outwards while hardening his mind against the blackness. His necklace began to glow hot with vibrating energy and he felt its pulse through his fingers. He imagined the white light spreading outwards and forming a ring around his home.

Next door, Jem's computer surged and he nearly lost his connection, the screen momentarily blacking out.

Downstairs his mother felt a strange sensation and although in mid-argument with her husband Alexander, she stopped mid-sentence and noticed for the first time the worry he had been wearing for months. She mouthed a silent, 'I'm sorry,' before moving towards him and hugging him.

Upstairs, Stevie felt the blackness recede like the tide of some deadly ocean lagoon. It didn't disappear entirely, but subsided enough for Stevie to think clearly and his first thought was the real perception of danger he was actually in. He knew, in his core, something was terribly wrong, just as surely he knew that he was hopelessly able to defend himself against it. His mindreading, his necklace and his basic knowledge of Illuminators were woefully inadequate. Like it or not, he had to begin to embrace his Illumination powers again…but more than that, he had to learn all he could, before it was too late.

Once again, he pushed his thoughts outward to his Aunt Bessie. "Please come, please come," he mouthed under his breath, for the second time that day.

Chapter Five

Mary Lou and the Shadowcasters

Mary Lou drove the bolt home on her front gate. Her dad wouldn't be home, she knew that. He would be at work, or meeting with that Devlin Hood's father. Oh yes, she knew all about the Hoods. How they had moved to town and were part of the plan to extend the Shadowcasters' influence in Valley Dale, like they did all over the country. She knew because she was the daughter of a Shadowcaster, but not one of them. She took after her mother's side of the family and had, with the support of Stevie's Aunt Bessie, secretly embraced her Illuminator heritage. Not that it was obvious to her father and his followers. No, she was good at keeping secrets. She had to be.

She put her backpack down on the hall table, and went to the kitchen for a quick snack, pulling out the peanut butter, bread and milk, her staple diet of late. Buttering the bread with thick wads of peanut butter and pouring a long, cold glass of milk, she retreated to her room. If she hurried, she would be able to take her motorbike out for a quick ride. Highly illegal, she knew, to be riding at only 13 years of age, but she kept to the long, winding tracks that began at the bush reserve at the back of her house. She was used to doing things by herself, had been since her mother had died. At first, after her mum's death, her dad had tried to build a relationship with her, trying to get close. But it was never going to work. They were as different as day is to night. And she just didn't agree with the way her father treated people. With him there was always an ulterior motive and she saw through that, even if others didn't.

Shadowcasters, Bessie had told her, always had an ulterior motive in everything they did and with everyone they met. It was all about recruitment, a subtle but persuasive influence to get under people's guards and win them over so that they would stay silent when they saw the first glimpses of how Shadowcasters work. After a time they even began helping the Shadowcasters, whether they knew it or not, or didn't admit it to themselves more likely.

With enough followers, they were able to increase their influence and continue to recruit people to their cause. They were not a cult – no they were everyday people from all walks of life dedicated to gaining power and when they got it, corruption always followed. An underground brethren sharing the common aim: that if enough influence was spread, there would not be enough good people left to take up the good fight. And when someone stood up to them, like the Vegas family, they came after them with a vengeance. The only reason they left Mary Lou alone was because she was the daughter of one of their inner circle. Her father was close to Chris Barron, as was Blake Hood, Devlin's father. As long as she kept her Illuminator work hidden from them, they would leave her alone. Although she had nothing in common with her father, she was his daughter nevertheless. She still hoped he would one day understand why she could not follow the Shadowcasters. He had loved her mother once, an Illuminator. She prayed that would be enough for herself and her dad, if he ever found out she was working against the Shadowcasters.

But for today, it was enough just to pull on her jeans and favorite T-shirt, lace up her bike boots and head for the garage to her motorbike. Wheeling it out the back gate and onto the bush track that led down to the ocean, she kick started the motor. It fired up on the first start and she clicked it into gear. She was off then, building up momentum and speeding through the gear changes. As she came into the corners she geared down and let her bike slide midway through them, so that she kept a steady pace. She would ride down as far as she could, to the little clearing beside the ocean lagoon. It was a good ride.

Weaving her way through the bush, she tested her skill and increased the pressure on the throttle, moving it up a notch. The back of the bike was sliding out, ever so slightly, but she knew she could sustain the pace. The wind rushed by her, and adrenalin pounded through her veins. She reached the lagoon in record time, but she was sweating from the concentration and energy required to ride fast and safe at the same time. She pulled into the clearing, turning her bike into a skid and cut the motor. It wasn't until she had taken her helmet off that she noticed a young man. She half thought about putting her helmet back on and riding off, but the Illuminator in her didn't sense any outward danger. When she looked more closely, she saw it was the taekwondo instructor, from Sun Lee's gym. He had recently come to the school to teach self-defense classes to the girls. She waved, but wondered what he was doing here, in her special spot.

He was sitting crossed legged beside the lagoon, looking out over the water. "What are you doing here?" she asked abruptly.

He turned very slowly toward her. "The same thing as you...finding my center."

She laughed, thinking to herself that riding a 250cc motorbike was about anything but peace.

"You laugh at me, but if you think about it, when you are riding your bike what happens to you when you are going at breakneck speed? With intense concentration you are finding the center of your being – at one with your machine and yourself. Well that is like my meditation, I am finding the source of power within myself, my center."

She nodded, understanding that to go within – meditate or deeply relax – was to tap into a power that no external source could match. She stared out over the lake noticing, for the first time since she arrived, the quiet of their surroundings.

"Umm, so you do understand. I'm glad you are here," he said. "My name is Bren Lee and I wanted to talk to you. That is why I came this afternoon."

She looked at him, startled by his premeditation.

"You knew I would be here. Are you following me?"

"No," he said, continuing to look out over the lake with a calm expression she thought he must always wear. "I came to talk to you about Stevie Vegas."

"Err, yeah. What about him. What is he to you?"

He turned to face her then. "To you I am just a gym instructor, Mary Lou. Yes I know your name and I also know more about you than you think."

She began to get up. This conversation was starting to alarm her.

"Please, sit down. I am your friend, and a friend to the Vegas family. Please…I mean you no harm, and I think I can be of assistance."

She sat back down. It wouldn't hurt to listen to him, hear him out anyway. And besides she was curious now. "OK…I'm listening."

"I know about the Illuminators and the Shadowcasters, and I know you are more Illuminator than Shadowcaster. It is simple really. There have always been forces for good and forces for evil. The battle is as ancient as the natural elements that formed this beautiful lake we see in front of us," he said.

"Are you an Illuminator too?" she asked, noticing the gentle strength within his face. This boy would be a worthy adversary to anyone.

"No. I am something different. My bloodline is old too, like the line of the Shadowcasters and Illuminators. My line is descended from the Samurai and, like you, my ancestors were of mixed blood – Japanese and Korean. I have the warrior code flowing deep within my veins and it is my code, my calling, to help those in need, and create an advantage so that balance can be achieved. We will never stop the spread of corrupt power. It breeds like a weed in a lake, destroying the natural beauty, so that even the sun's rays enable it to grow. Once that weed takes hold, it spreads outward and what was once growing strong and true, begins to die only to be replaced by that weed. Eventually, you are unable to see the bright surface of the lake. You only see the weed."

Mary Lou understood perfectly. She had long witnessed the congregating, planning and deliberate motivations of the Shadowcasters. From her place in the background, she had listened and studied their ways, all the while contacting Aunt Bessie when she could – passing information on. She knew if she was caught that not even her father's protection would be enough. But she did it anyway, overcoming her fear, in honor of her mother. It is what her mum would have done, what she would have wanted. She understood it when Bren Lee talked about honor. She understood it well.

"How can we help Stevie Vegas?" she said, without taking her eyes of the lake.

He turned to her, his face set with determination.

"He is far from ready. You know already what they are trying to do. It's revenge and vindication they are after. The Barrons are coming for him. Make no mistake about that, but before they come, they will weaken the Vegas family, make them vulnerable until at last, Stevie will succumb to their influence, or risk being destroyed."

"But what can we do? I don't know enough about Illuminator ways. My mother…she…I was only three when she passed away in a 'supposed accident.' I only know what Stevie's Aunt Bessie has told me."

"I believe we can help him. I will begin his training, disciplining his mind and teaching him how to put up the defenses he will need in the coming weeks," Bren Lee said.

Mary Lou nodded. "And I will contact my old friend Bessie Orion to tell her she can no longer delay coming to Valley Dale."

Chapter Six

Against the Odds

Stevie entered Sun Lee's gym that day with a lot on his mind. He had sent out his thoughts to Aunt Bessie, urging her to come to Valley Dale but, so far, he had not heard anything from her. Last night he had discovered that with the power of his thought, he could at least block out the darkness. He just didn't know why a white light surrounding his home would not only ease his nightmares, and dissipate the fog surrounding his thoughts, but ease the tension that had been hanging over the Vegas household. What he really needed was someone he could talk to. He knew now that it was not an option to shut his Illuminator powers off. He was being attacked by situations and people he could not see coming. His nightmares, the day in the schoolyard, the ever present blackness that hung over his home…he knew intuitively that he was under threat from the Shadowcasters and he had reached a point of no return. Either he had to defend himself and his family, or take more of what was being thrust at him; and Stevie Vegas was not used to lying down to threats and intimidation. Last night as he sat on his bed, pushing out the white light, his thoughts had become clear. He was going to change everything for his family – no more bad luck. He would make sure the Vegas family came out on top for once.

As he pushed open the door to the gym and accustomed his eyes to its usual dimness – Sun Lee never lit up his gym brightly, preferring a subdued natural light – he felt slightly more confident than he had in days. He finally understood what he had to do and in making that decision, he became more determined, calmer and resolved. Ahead, Bren Lee was kickboxing in the practice ring. He stopped at the ropes, watching the young man go through his moves. There was no doubt Bren Lee could fight, he thought. He would be a good trainer. Watching Bren Lee was like observing the wind in the trees, moving consistently with an undercurrent of power, lightning fast in the moment but gentle at times too. As Bren Lee kicked and weaved with his opponent, landing a blow when least expected, Stevie was reminded of when he skated using his intuition, becoming one with something higher than himself – Bren Lee was doing the same thing, only through the skill he possessed as a martial arts champion.

The bell rang, signaling the end of the sparring session. Stevie cleared his throat to try to get Bren Lee's attention. To his surprise the martial arts instructor gave him a warm smile. "Stevie Vegas, thank you for coming. I haven't forgotten our training session. But where is your brother?"

"Oh, Jem," Stevie said almost crossly. "He's at home on his computer, again. He said he had a headache, but you know how it is with gaming, they hardly ever come out of their rooms and always have an excuse for not doing something. I'm sorry, Bren Lee. I know you were expecting him."

Bren Lee wiped the sweat off his brow with a towel. "That's OK, Stevie, no problem."

He motioned for Stevie to enter the ring. "We'll train together today and I'll give you one on one instruction. First I want you to sit quietly in the middle of the ring. Yes, that's right, cross your legs. I want you to let go of your thoughts today."

"But aren't we going to kickbox...I saw you, you're good. I want to learn how to do that..."

Bren Lee sat down beside him and gave him a knowing smile. "Yes, I know you're eager to learn how to fight, but first you need to learn how to clear your mind and focus only on a single thought...and to go with the natural flow and rhythm of your spirit."

Stevie rolled his eyes. He had done enough thinking and today he wanted action. And what was this flow thing? As if reading his mind, Bren Lee put his finger up to stop any more thought, or talk. Bren Lee walked over to a nearby CD player at the ring's edge and clicked the 'on' button. Immediately the sounds of Eastern music began to infiltrate the gym, which Stevie noticed, was empty.

"You're puzzled no doubt, Stevie?"

"Yes, just a little. I don't mean to be rude but I came here to learn self-defense, not to listen to music…"

"And listen and learn about self-defense you will," Bren Lee said, sitting down opposite him. "I want you to empty your mind and concentrate only on a single flame. In your mind's eye, watch that flame as it grows brighter…"

"But—" Stevie said, almost desperately now.

"Quiet, Stevie…imagine the flame."

Stevie closed his eyes, knowing that it was useless to protest. He listened to the sound of the music, which he thought sounded like a river flowing. He did as he was told and imagined a single bright flame. The sound of Bren Lee's voice began to grow dimmer.

"See that flame, how it moves with a gentle breeze, yet it leaps and darts as though it is ready to burn more brightly at any given moment. It is growing stronger now, Stevie, as you are growing stronger. See the colors in the flame: blue at its base, and yellow at its tip, the hottest part of the flame, and the white light that surrounds the flame. Let yourself drift, Stevie, and become one with flame…."

Stevie had no sense of time passing, only the steady sound of Bren Lee's voice, which seemed far off and distant. He was immersed in the flame, and he noticed how it dipped and wove as if it was a living thing. The white light, the symbol of the Illuminator, began to grow brighter around its edges so that soon, Stevie imagined, it was filling the whole of the gym and he was at its center. The floor beneath him vibrated and he felt he was being lifted out of the ring and skyward. He heard Bren

Lee's far off voice, "Make your mind your friend…fill it with the living, heart of the flame and let nothing else penetrate. Surround yourself in the pure, white light of the flame which is growing stronger now, as you are, Stevie Vegas…"

As he imagined himself as the flame, he felt the unease and worry of the past weeks leave him. At that moment the fear of the unknown left him too, and he was conscious that this fear had been obstructing his power and eroding his confidence. From this new vantage point, he could see clearly that the Shadowcasters were at the heart of his unease, and were growing stronger. But he was growing stronger; he was the white light and the living, heart of the flame. He had no fear, only the will, growing stronger inside, to become who he was meant to be. To become an Illuminator.

"I want you now to bring yourself back to the gym." Bren Lee's voice was gentle and persuasive. Stevie concentrated on Bren Lee's hypnotic suggestion, took a deep breath and opened his eyes. Bren Lee was still sitting opposite him, a smile on his face, and happiness in his eyes.

"Well, Stevie Vegas, how was that. Still think learning kickboxing is the only way to defend yourself?"

Stevie smiled to himself. "No," he said simply. And in that moment he used his Illuminator powers to read Bren Lee's thoughts. In those thoughts he found friendship and, surprisingly, knowledge of the Illuminators.

"You know?" Stevie asked.

"Yes."

And there was no more to be said. Whatever Bren Lee was, Stevie knew implicitly he could trust him.

"We will stop the Shadowcasters, Bren Lee," he said.

"Yes, Stevie, they will not win, but you need to become strong as an Illuminator and, yes, we will now have a session in the ring. I will show you how to make your body the servant of your mind."

With that, Bren Lee got up and assumed the self-defense position. Instinctively, Stevie assumed the attack position and launched at him with a kick.

Bren Lee moved gently to the side. "No Stevie, you mustn't signal so obviously you are going to attack. Assume a neutral position, but be ready to attack. That way your opponent will be put off guard. Still your mind, become the flame and be ready to leap and move like the wind."

Stevie stood still and imagined the flame and the white light spreading outward into the ring. It formed a circle around him, like a fortress. Bren Lee launched his attack, a kick to his shoulder, but Stevie's arm intuitively moved to knock his leg sideways. Bren Lee stumbled and, at that moment, Stevie launched his kick, aiming for his legs.

But Bren Lee was a master and in a split second had caught his balance and was standing upright, aiming a kick, this time, at Stevie's back. Like the flame, Stevie moved with alertness, sideways, managing to deflect the kick. Bren Lee laughed.

"Ah…so you are a quick learner, Stevie Vegas."

Stevie resumed his neutral position and waited for more training.

"That's all for today, Stevie," Bren said, bowing deeply to him.

Stevie bowed in response. "Thank you," he said, his voice full of gratitude.

"You're welcome."

Stevie skated home from Sun Lee's gym. He had so much to tell Jem, having resolved to try to mend the growing distance with his brother. After all, this was Jem, his childhood friend and partner. The moods – Jem's sullenness – he thought optimistically would all be a thing of the past. He executed a grind on the rail going down the stairs to Hill Street, like he had done a million times before. He tore through the front door, ignoring his mother's hellos and took the steps two at a time to Jem's room.

Opening the door, he saw that his brother was at his usual place in front of his computer.

"Jem!" Stevie yelled. "I've got so much to tell you. That Bren Lee is awesome, you gotta come to see him tomorrow…"

Jem turned to face Stevie, his face expressionless. It was only then that Stevie saw the black aura surrounding his brother – the dark shards shooting upward into the air surrounding them.

"No, Jem! No!"

Chapter Seven

Out of the Fire and Almost into Flames

Stevie blinked hard in Jem's room, hoping against hope that the black shards, so much a part of a Shadowcaster's aura, were a trick of the light. Perhaps he was tired from the training with Bren Lee, but opening his eyes wide, he still saw the black halo surrounding Jem.

"Jem, step away from the computer for a minute. Come over here. I want to talk to you," Stevie said, motioning to the bed. He sat down, waiting for Jem to speak, still watching that deathly aura. As Jem started to move toward him, the blackness faded and, once sitting on the bed, it had turned to a dull shade of grey – a Greycaster, neither fully Shadowcaster nor Illuminator, Stevie thought.

"What have you been doing?" he asked Jem, trying to keep reason in his voice.

"Nothing. Playing Vision Quest with my new friend."

"And who is that?" Stevie asked, knowing before Jem answered that this 'new friend' was no such thing.

"A boy I met the other day, lives next door actually, but he's my friend not yours. Stick to your stupid girlfriend for all I care."

"Hang on a minute, Jem," Stevie said, ignoring the taunt at his and Mary Lou's friendship. "Who is the boy next door and how did you meet him?"

Jem's face took on a stubborn expression. "My friend, my new friend's name is Devlin Hood and he is an avatar on Vision Quest. In fact, we are recruiting new members into our team and pretty soon we are going to be at the top ranking. I might not be able to skate like you, Stevie, but I am good at gaming and to some people that does matter. We are not all skating freaks like you."

Stevie was about to say, 'Yes, but you're all night crawlers on a stupid, little machine hour after hour, when you should be getting outside like other kids,' but he didn't. He knew it was pointless to inflame the situation. Looking at Jem's hardened expression, he wondered how he hadn't noticed they were growing apart. Like everything else lately, things had gone from bad to worse, and he had been too busy resisting his Illuminator powers, and thinking of himself, to notice.

"Jem, I know you are good at lots of things. You don't need a computer game to prove anything," he said.

Jem went to get up. "That is so typical of you, Stevie. You don't know what you're talking about. I don't want to play soccer any more. That's for babies. If you got off that skateboard for long enough, you'd see that everyone plays Vision Quest."

Stevie nodded, resisting the urge to argue with Jem and instead said, "OK, then. Maybe you're right. Tell me about Vision Quest. What is it and what's the point of the game."

Jem sat back down again pleased Stevie was taking an interest in something he liked. Stevie noticed the grey aura dimming and breathed an inward sigh of relief.

"Right. Vision Quest is a game of strategy. Yes, it's a war game, but to get anywhere, you have to be able to think about how you're going to bring down your opponent before they bring you down. It's taught me a lot about things, you know."

Stevie tried hard to understand where Jem was coming from. It was so alien to him that Jem would be talking about bringing anyone down. "Why do you need to learn that sort of thing Jem, you never used to think like that before? I remember when kicking a soccer ball round our backyard and trying to outwit me and the neighbors was enough."

Jem's eyes hardened again. "You would say that, wouldn't you, Stevie. You wouldn't know what it was like to be smaller than everyone else, to be someone's younger brother, and not get any of the attention." He glared at Stevie, with real anger in his eyes. "No you wouldn't know what it's like to live in someone else's shadow, to always be the one that needed sticking up for, to be the easy target. You wouldn't know that would you, Mr. Skater extraordinaire."

Stevie was about to say that he wasn't some skating guru and that Jem was more important to him than any skateboarder, but he heard his mum's urgent tones echoing up the stairwell.

"Dinner. Jem, Stevie, dinner's on the table and we've got a guest. Come down now please."

Instead he said, "Jem, we'll finish this later. It's important. We need to talk about this…"

"Maybe," Jem answered, as he got up and ran down the stairs, as if further talk was completely unnecessary.

Stevie sat for a minute, aware his mum was serving dinner at the table. He glanced over at the computer screen, and saw that it was emitting a dark light. He knew without even being told that Jem's new friend Devlin Hood was somehow to blame for all of this. Outside Jem's window, was the upstairs window of one of the Hood's bedrooms. He wondered if it was Devlin's. He thought back to the start of his nightmares, around the same time the Hood's had moved in next door. What were they? Who were they? And why were they here? Questions…and Stevie knew he didn't have nearly enough answers.

"Stevie. Stevie Vegas. Dinner is on the table, *now*!" his mum yelled.

He took the stairs two at a time, half jumping, and half sliding down the banister. Entering the dining room, he noticed an extra place set for the visitor, just as his mum and Aunt Bessie came in carrying hot, steaming dishes of chicken casserole and rice. "Aunt Bessie!" he cried. "Thank God you're here…at last."

His dad, who was sitting at the head of the table, looked up in surprise. "Stevie? What do you mean by 'at last'? You sound almost desperate to see Aunt Bessie."

Stevie shot a look at Jem, but he was wearing that same blank expression he went around with most of the time these days.

"Umm…no, I mean…I've missed Aunt Bessie. It's been about six months since we last saw her. I just miss her. OK."

His mum smiled. "Of course, you do, we all do." She gave her aunt a huge hug.

Aunt Bessie had her usual merry smile on her face and her eyes were full of laughter, and Stevie noticed, happiness. "It's so nice, Vegas family, to be welcomed so warmly." She glanced around at each member in turn, taking everything in. When she got to Jem, she paused momentarily, a brief look of worry creasing her forehead, and then she looked directly at Stevie. He heard her thoughts, "We will talk later tonight. There are urgent matters I need to discuss with you, but for now let's enjoy this precious family time while we can."

Stevie nodded ever so slightly to her.

"OK, Vegas family," his mother said brightly. "Let's eat and it's Jem's favorite tonight, Chicken a la Orange."

Jem frowned. "Used to be, Mum, like when I was eight. I am twelve now, you know."

Aunt Bessie was the first to reply. "Well, young man, I'm sixty-three and I've still an appetite for Chicken a la Orange casserole. It used to be, and still is my favorite."

Jem smiled then, his old smile, and Stevie noticed the grey aura was very faint. Around Aunt Bessie now, it was almost disappearing. He wondered if she noticed it.

His aunt spooned a generous helping onto Jem's plate. "Here you go, plenty of the orange sauce, just the way you like it."

"Thanks, Aunt Bessie," he said, smiling brightly at her. "And I'm really glad you're here too."

They sat down at the table and enjoyed a simple family meal. As Stevie looked around from face to face, he noticed that the tension had lifted from the Vegas household. Not even the closeness of the Hoods next door could dent the spirit of family togetherness tonight.

Stevie noticed that Jem's grey aura had completely disappeared. And the dark clouds that had seemingly hung over him
were gone too. He glanced at Aunt Bessie. She was talking to his
mum, her favorite niece. His mum was nodding eagerly and
smiling. Yes, all would be well now Aunt Bessie was around. He
sighed almost contentedly, and began to tuck into his Chicken a
la Orange.

Chapter Eight

An Illuminator's Light

The Vegas household was quiet when Stevie and his aunt decided to walk that evening. Jem was watching a movie with Mum and Dad; the Vegas' two dogs and one cat curled up in baskets and on lounges in the TV room. The lights had been dimmed, and the family were relaxing after a happy and unexpectedly joyful meal. It was as if Aunt Bessie's presence had restored the family in some way. The dark clouds that had hovered over them, were miraculously gone, for an evening at least. Stevie hoped forever. But he knew that life seldom yielded in such a gracious manner without a price being paid first. What was that price, he wondered, and who would have to pay?

"It's not you, darling, who will pay the price," his aunt said, placing a protective arm around him as they walked. "You've done nothing wrong, nor do you or any of my family deserve it when bad things happen."

Stevie glanced at her and was glad, yet again, for his good luck in having such an aunt.

They were strolling along Hetherington Avenue, a short block from Elm Street. It hadn't been hard to leave the house that night for their walk. Aunt Bessie said she needed to stretch her legs and his mum and dad had jumped at the chance to stay in with Jem. He knew they too were worried by Jem's self-imposed exile from the family to game away the long hours of an evening.

Stevie kicked at the stones underfoot. "Well, then, why is this happening to us?" He gave his aunt a direct stare, demanding honesty from her.

She sighed and slowed her step. She seemed to choose her words carefully. "Stevie, this isn't just happening to you, don't think that God or someone else has singled you out for all the bad luck this world can muster. For as old as time is itself, there have been those who have battled against those who seek to do evil in this world. And evil comes in many disguises. You know what your biggest armor is against it?"

"My Illuminator powers?" Stevie answered.

"No," Aunt Bessie said, placing her hand on his heart. "It is the goodness in your heart, Stevie, that gives you the most power. That is where your Illuminator powers live. Not in your mind, but in your heart."

Stevie silently shook his head. "If that's right, Aunt Bessie, then why do bad things happen to good people? Tell me that much."

They were coming up to Elm Street and his aunt slowed her pace.

"Let's rest awhile here, Stevie," she said. "I don't like this street...ah, yes, I know who lives here, I have been in constant communication with Mary Lou, but her father's energy is strong, and there's something new...coming from that house on the hill."

Stevie noticed, for the first time, the stately home at the top of Elm Street. There were moving vans outside. Funny, he hadn't given the dark, old place a second thought when he first visited Mary Lou, intent only on the Shadowcaster energy emanating from her own place when her father was inside.

His aunt interrupted his thoughts. "Now, back to your question, Stevie. Why do bad things happen to good people – you mean why are the bad things happening to you and your family?"

"Let's sit for a minute," she said, taking a seat at the nearby, empty Elm Street bus stop.

Stevie sat down next to her, but his gaze was transfixed on the old home on the hill. It felt like it was drawing him to it.

"Stevie, I'm not excusing this world," his aunt said, bringing him back to the present moment. "No one can. There are things that have happened; things I have seen that sometimes make me question why I continue to use my Illuminator powers for good. I have been so close to creating chaos for Shadowcasters, of attacking them at night in their dreams like they do us. Of evening the score. But you know, I always come back to why we are here, why there are two opposing forces, Illuminators and Shadowcasters, and that is to keep the balance of good and evil in this world. And the choice is always ours. When the bad things happen, as they do through no fault of our own, which side do you want to be on? The side that causes more bad things to happen to other innocent people who do no wrong and through no fault of their own are targets, or the side that helps stop the bad things from happening."

Stevie thought about what his aunt said. He didn't answer at first and the silence lingered, while he took on her words and acknowledged the truth of them.

After a while, Stevie spoke. "You know, Aunt Bessie, I hear you; I really do. But I'm just a skateboarder. I didn't ask for any of this to happen. I don't want to hurt anyone with my powers, and I don't want to take on the Shadowcasters. I just want to be left alone. I want things to go back to the way they were before I became an Illuminator. I don't want much, just to be left alone."

His aunt sighed. "Stevie, what do you think makes you so brilliant on a skateboard. It's because you're tapping into your instincts, your intuition and your power to create. When you skate, you are using your Illuminator powers. We don't ask for our talents or skills, it's who we are and, sometimes, because of those talents, other people notice us and want what we have, because taking away our power means they have power themselves...well at least they think it will lead to power for themselves. Sometimes, we have to defend ourselves and more often than not, we have to be ahead of the attack. And where we can, we need to be above the attack...stepping outside of it and not letting it corrupt us in any way. But I'll ask you again, which side do you want to be on? The side that protects or the side that causes pain, anguish and grief? Don't answer me now. Think on it awhile."

Stevie met his aunt's gaze and saw the love she had for him. He knew she only wanted what was best for him.

"Thanks, Aunt Bessie. I don't mean to be a coward or anything, it's just—"

"—that you're a 13-year-old boy who wants a normal life," his aunt said, interrupting him mid-sentence.

"A normal life…now that would be something wouldn't it."

His aunt laughed, with just a hint of mischief in her eyes. "Oh, I don't think either you or me would be satisfied with that."

They got up and continued walking, aware it was going on 8 pm and beginning to get dark.

"If you don't mind, Stevie, let's not walk down Elm Street tonight. I really don't like the look of those big old trees. Rather ghostly I think."

Stevie placed a reassuring hand on her arm. "You won't get any argument from me, Aunt Bessie. Tonight, I just want us to be a normal family."

They walked slowly back to the Vegas house. Just as they were nearing the Hood residence, his aunt stumbled. "Stevie, I can feel the energy coming from that place. It's not good. If I'm not mistaken it's as I suspected. It's the energy of a Shadowcaster or worse still, a number of Shadowcasters. I knew as much. Promise me you will think over what I've said tonight because if you're willing, we will need to begin your Illuminator training in earnest."

"My training," Stevie asked, shocked at the urgency in her voice.

"Yes, you have a lot to learn about the powers of Illuminators. Much to learn…and there is no time left."

"Left?" Stevie asked, opening the door for his aunt.

"Enough said for tonight, Stevie. Tonight you get your wish to be a normal family. There is only love and light tonight for the Vegas family, and the sweetest of dreams for you, young man."

"Umm, now that would be nice…for a change. But how?

"A protective light of course, around your house. Now we Illuminators are very good for some things."

Stevie paused at the doorway. "Seriously, Aunt Bessie, I will think over what you said. Can I let you know in the next few days?"

"Of course you can, darling. I will be here for you, for as long as you need me."

He reached up and gave her a huge hug, saying simply, "Thank you."

Aunt Bessie hugged her nephew tight. "Remember, light and dark, shades of grey – we are what our choices make us."

With that, they closed the door on the outside world to feel the simple joy of being a family.

Chapter Nine

A Midnight Ride

Stevie woke to the sound of pebbles landing squarely on his windowpane. The moon was full and the night unusually light. At first he thought he was dreaming, a dream where someone was knocking loudly and insistently on his front door. He rolled over hoping in his dream-like state they would go away. But the knock only became louder until he forced his eyes open to focus on the sound. Thump, another pebble landed on the window.

Keep that up and the window will break, he thought. He got up from his bed to investigate. Down below, silhouetted in the moonlight was Mary Lou Nova.

He hoisted the window open.

"Hey, what are you doing? Want to wake my mum and dad?"

"Sorry, Stevie, but I need to talk to you."

"Now, for God's sake? It's the middle of the night. Haven't you ever heard of sleep?"

Her tone was more urgent now.

"Of course I have, Stevie Vegas. But this can't wait. Hurry up will you."

Stevie opened his window enough to maneuver his body through it, grab a foothold on the nearby drainpipe, and climb down.

"OK, here I am. Middle of the night and all. Now what is it?

Mary Lou was dressed in jeans and her leather jacket, despite the mildness of the night. Stevie noticed she had her bike boots on. On the other hand, he was still in his pajamas.

"You'll need to get dressed," she said. "We can't talk here. I've got my bike in the side street. If you're game, I'll take you for a ride."

"And why would I go riding with you in the middle of the

night?" he said, wondering what had got into her.

Her brown eyes flashed, and Stevie finally understood that what brought her to the Vegas household at midnight, must have been vitally important.

"I think you know already, Stevie, I'm not prone to dramatics, but what I've got to tell you...well show you...can't wait."

"OK," he said, his tone serious now. "Give me a minute."

When he returned he was in jeans and a long sleeve T-shirt. He'd also brought his jacket with him, knowing she meant to take him somewhere on the bike. He wasn't sure about that part of it; he had never ridden with her before...well anyone for that matter.

"You'll go easy, eh?" he said as they wheeled the bike into a deserted street nearby.

"Yeah," she said. "'Bout as easy as you do on your skateboard on a good night."

He laughed despite the fact it was the middle of the night and he was being taken for a ride on a motorbike – not something he wanted to do, even in daylight.

She kicked the bike over and he swung his leg over the back to ride pillion. And then she was off, as silently as her 250cc would allow her. Weaving through the deserted streets, she took a side turn to the Valley Dale reserve. Once on the dirt, she opened the throttle up and their pace increased. Stevie felt confident as her passenger though, knowing with certainty that Mary Lou could ride...and like the wind.

They took the trails behind Valley Dale, and in the direction of Elm Street, until they came to a rocky hill. She cut the motor.

"We'll have to walk from here," she said, getting off the bike and taking off her helmet.

He was about to protest and demand more information before they embarked on their rocky climb, but something in the way she began climbing – steadfast and quickly, kept him quiet. Instead, he followed her lead until they reached the summit.

Standing beside her, the view was spectacular and he could see almost the whole of Valley Dale.

At first he didn't see what she wanted him to see – only the dim street lights and occasional house lights below. He looked over to her, waiting for her to speak, but Mary Lou's gaze was fixed firmly on the old hillside house in Elm Street.

Stevie didn't notice it at first, but the longer he looked, the more he began to see why she had brought him here. Dark clouds swirled above the old house and Stevie noticed the black shards shooting skywards. It was as if the devil of demons lived there, and Stevie knew, or thought he knew, that there were no such things.

"There," she pointed, to the huge stone entrance.

Stevie strained his eyes and could only just make out the lettering on the gates. With a sickening feeling in his stomach, he knew even before he read them what they would say.

'Barron estate,' in large, imposing letters was lit by powerful floodlights.

He gulped the night air down, which had turned extremely cold. A chill wind had sprung up and it seemed to penetrate through his jacket. The first thought that came into his head was the warning he'd heard on the wind, like voices from behind a dark veil. "They are coming for you…"

Stevie Vegas knew now, that as much as he had tried to escape his past, there could be no reprieve, not now or ever. As long as the Barrons were on his trail, there was only one place to go, and that was to the heart of his Illuminator powers.

"Breathe," Mary Lou whispered into the night air.

He took in long, deep breaths and was silent as the seconds ticked over to minutes. All he could do was stare at the swirling, dark mass over the Barron estate and try to think. He didn't know where it came from, but in his moment of near despair at being thrust into the Shadowcasters' web yet again, a voice reached up from deep inside. It was his own, clear and true, and strong.

He straightened and looked directly at Mary Lou. All around the night seemed to close in on them, as even the full moon became lost behind the dark clouds. He held her gaze and she looked directly back at him. They searched each other's thoughts until one very dominant thought crystallized and he knew then that she was his friend, and that she knew everything there was to know about him.

"And so it is," he thought. "They have returned. Well, let them. I've got nothing and no one to fear."

She smiled at him then. "Good to hear," she said aloud. "And if it means anything at all to you, I'll be there for you. And there are others who can be counted on. You won't be alone, Stevie Vegas."

He returned her smile, the intensity of his resolve slipping away to calm assuredness.

"One thing is for sure," he said speaking aloud. "I'll need to learn all I can about my Illuminator powers now. You know about Illuminators don't you?"

She nodded.

He smiled at her. "Can't have the Barrons or the Shadowcasters on the loose in Valley Dale; they'll turn the place into a writhing, demonic mess."

Mary Lou laughed. "Trust you, Stevie Vegas – just how deep is that air of bravado of yours?"

He was quick to respond. "Ask me after a few training sessions with Aunt Bessie."

Chapter 10

A Light Grows Brighter

Stevie slept fitfully that night, anxious for the morning light, and to tell his aunt what he knew – that his Illuminator training should begin that day. He had deliberately not thought about the Barrons' arrival in Valley Dale. Was it Jacob Barron or his father Chris, or both? He had reasoned that it didn't matter who was on his doorstep; it would take all his skill and the combined power of all the Illuminators he knew…well himself, Mary Lou and Aunt Bessie. And of course he knew he could count on Bren Lee.

As he tossed and turned, he tried to reason with himself knowing he was hopelessly out maneuvered by the Shadowcasters. If ever there was a rite of passage, it was that night before the sun rose when his darkest fears haunted him. A million thoughts ran through his mind, but the most overriding one was the reality of his situation. Short of a miracle, he didn't know how it would end and he feared the worst. There was little hope on the horizon that night.

He calculated that the Barrons, who were the head Shadowcasting family, had brought with them more Shadowcasters, outnumbering the few Illuminators in Valley Dale that he knew of. There were the Hoods of course, and Mary Lou's father. Who else lurked in the shadows unknown to him? Shadowcasters like others who lived and breathed the need to acquire more power, gathered like minds around them in numbers. That way they were sure of their victory by outnumbering a weaker target, and then isolating that target, just as the Vegas family was being isolated now.

That night Stevie Vegas thought well beyond his 13 years. Through fate, or more importantly, his birthright, he had been catapulted into a position of power. He knew he wasn't ready for it. In the middle of the night, when panic threatened to overtake him, he listened to his inner voice – as he had many times at the skatepark, in the middle of a particularly difficult aerial or jump. It was the voice of confidence that defeated his fear; that despite the odds there would be a way to triumph. And at the heart of the thought was determination – a dogged determination to win against those odds.

By the time the morning sun rose over the hills of Valley Dale, Stevie Vegas had accepted he would have to face the Barrons again, and that training and preparation were his only hope. Like he went into any major skateboarding tournament, with confidence and the right amount of careful assessment and knowing the risks, he began to strategize. And his prime strategy was to learn all he could about his Illuminator powers. It was time to begin.

He rushed through his school lessons that day, hardly able to concentrate on them, and hurried home. His Aunt Bessie was with his mum in the kitchen making chocolate cake for dessert. He winked at her when he came in.

"Hi, Mum. Hi, Aunt Bessie. What's for dinner?"

His mum handed him the chocolate covered beaters from the Mixmaster, which he took with eager anticipation. Chocolate was exactly what he wanted.

"How was school?" his mum said.

"Oh, you know, the usual…actually I was wondering if I could borrow Aunt Bessie for a few hours?"

Sylvia Vegas looked puzzled. "For what?"

"Well, I've got to go down to Sun Lee's gym, for a quick training session and I was wondering if she could drive me. That way I…we can be back in time for dinner."

Stevie automatically crossed his fingers. He didn't like lying to his mum, but he didn't see any other way they could get out of the house unnoticed.

His Aunt Bessie had almost finished washing up the mixing

bowls. "It's Ok, Stevie. I've already told your mum that's what we'll be doing. And she's OK with it, aren't you, Sylvia?"

Sylvia popped the cake in the oven, taking out a steaming tray of moussaka.

"Sure, dinner's cooked already. You two go ahead. But don't be late. I want us all to eat together, like we did last night, as a family. And I don't want your aunt away for too long either. It's not often she can take time off from her travels to come and visit."

Before too long Stevie and Aunt Bessie were heading out the door to the Vegas family's Ford Territory.

"Hey," Stevie said, 'how'd you know that's what I was going to say, before I said it?"

His aunt turned the key in the ignition and the Ford sprang into life.

"That, my boy, is part of my Illuminator powers. Although you will find this hard to take in at the moment, I can see the future at times and coupled with the practical knowledge that you do go down to Sun Lee's to train after school, it was enough. Sometimes when we use our intuition with our powers of logic, we do end up with the right answers. Of course, there was a chance you might make another excuse, but it was worth the gamble. That's the other thing, Stevie; you have to know when to take that gamble that you will be right. It's no use doubting yourself."

Stevie grinned at his aunt, realizing there was a lot he had to learn.

"OK, Aunt Bessie, as usual you're right. Where are we off too?"

"Actually, I am taking you to Walnut Grove. Most Valley Dale residents know it as a seaside reserve, where families can picnic but, in actual fact, Stevie, it is one of the many sacred sites in this area and draws great power from the earth. I want to show you how nature can work for you to protect you and help you…among other things."

Aunt Bessie negotiated the reserve's trails down to the seaside, cutting the Ford's engines when they reached a huge circle of trees – mighty Oaks and huge Walnut trees. The grounds were deserted, apart from a family that was packing up to leave after a swim in the nearby river, which had forged a path through the hills behind Valley Dale and down to the sea.

They sat for a few minutes in the Ford and Stevie waited for his aunt to speak.

"Stevie, by now you know that Chris Barron has brought his son Jacob to Valley Dale, and they have moved into the old mansion on Elm Street."

Stevie nodded.

"Mary Lou showed me last night…It's OK, Aunt Bessie, really it is. You don't have to worry about me."

Aunt Bessie put her hand up to silence him.

"I'm not worried about you, my boy. Nothing could be further from the truth, but I will say this, you have a long way to go in your training. Up until now, you have been resisting your Illuminator powers and resisting who you are. You're not like other thirteen-year-old boys. You must know that you're different…and it's no good wasting time wishing you were someone else. Do you understand, Stevie?"

"I guess. I just wanted all the bad stuff to go away, that's all. And yes, for a long time I wished I was like other kids my age. It's not easy being different – feeling different – from everyone else."

She smiled her warmest of smiles. "I know, Stevie. I remember when I was your age and wished for the same thing. But you know what? Sitting here now at sixty-three years of age, having spent my life as an Illuminator, I can tell you that the upsides far outweigh the downsides. There is magic to be found in life, Stevie, and as an Illuminator you are on the edges of it. At any time you just need to step into that world. And the Shadowcasters…well, it's not all bad. Once you learn how to master your fear and tap into your natural powers, your natural self, you will no longer be at a disadvantage. Before I start your training, Stevie, I need to know that you will not resist the light that grows within you. You need to embrace who you are, and all that you will become."

Stevie knew his aunt was right, he had been resisting his Illuminator powers and while he fought against his true nature, not acknowledging who he was, he would never move forward. He was done with hiding away and trying to please everyone all the time: his teachers, his friends, and even his parents. It was time his mum and dad knew who and what he was. And it was time to stop hiding or apologizing for his talents, to Jem, to his friends and at school. It was time to step forward, out of the shadows.

He nodded to his aunt, who had been waiting for his answer.

"I won't resist who I am," he said. "I want you to show me that…who I am."

"I can show you your Illuminator powers and how to use them, but you alone can only discover who you are. But, I can tell you this, Stevie, once you know, you'll never forget."

He grinned at her. "Righto, Aunt Bessie, let's get started…on me."

Leaving the Ford parked in the clearing, Stevie and his aunt made their way into the forest. Stevie felt a slight breeze spring up, which rustled the leaves of the Oaks, as though they were whispering of his arrival. He could hear the faint sounds of the nearby river and noticed, for the first time, the bird life that inhabited the forest.

Everywhere, the forest was alive with sights and sounds. In front of him, a group of orange butterflies wove their way through the grass and the flowers, and eventually caught the current of the breeze. Funny, he hadn't noticed much about nature before, spending most of his time at the skatepark. To him, nature meant hills and dips and places to build concrete and metal, the two things that he could skate on. But in the forest with Aunt Bessie, it was different. He noticed the sun on his face and, most of all, he noticed the wind. It was as if the wind captured his thoughts and responded to them.

"Aunt Bessie," he whispered. "This might sound stupid, but I was wondering…umm…what's with the wind?"

His aunt, who was walking a few paces in front, stopped and turned around. Stevie noticed she was smiling that smile, not patronizing no, but a smile that said she knew exactly what he meant.

"You notice the wind? That's good. You were meant to, and yes, it is responding to you. Nearly there."

She stopped, looking around. "Yes, this will do nicely."

Stevie noticed they were in the center of a huge circle of trees again. But this time, there was something different. He felt as though the trees and the wind were expecting him, and now that he had arrived, were waiting…for something.

His aunt sat down on a nearby log and motioned for him to sit opposite her. He sat on a green, lush patch of grass in front and looked expectantly at her. She closed her eyes and after a few moments appeared to be in trance. He noticed, rather apprehensively, that the wind picked up; it was no longer a breeze.

As if from far away, Aunt Bessie projected her thoughts, telling him to close his eyes and to feel the wind on his cheek and to imagine it becoming stronger. Instinctively, Stevie raised his arms to the wind and to his utter surprise, it reacted to him. It became stronger, moving the branches of the nearby trees. At first he doubted it was his doing, but in imagining the wind becoming stronger, it did. He could doubt it no more. He had created a windstorm, gentle as it was, but a windstorm nevertheless.

"Good, Stevie," his aunt murmured. "You are learning that you can control the elements. Earth, wind and water, are all a part of you and you can communicate with them. Now I want you to focus your thoughts on the rays of the sun."

Stevie's hand went immediately to his necklace.

"I want you to imagine the light of the sun becoming brighter and forming a circle around you. Let the light move through you, from head to toe, become one with the light."

Stevie did as he was instructed. He imagined the light of the sun entering the top of his head and exiting at his feet to form a brilliant circle around him. At that moment he felt an upward surge of power from the ground that penetrated every nerve and fiber of his body. Like the sensation of pure light in the gym that day with Bren Lee, Stevie became the light. But something else was happening to him in the forest with Aunt Bessie. Within the light he thought he could see events unfolding. He didn't know whether they were occurring in the immediate future, but he recognized the Valley Dale skatepark. Immediately, a thought came into his mind. "Don't try for the 900." He was puzzled. The 900 (degrees) was a skateboarding trick – a two and a half revolution, aerial spin. It was the trick that had nearly cost Jacob Barron his life. He let himself come out of the trance, only to see his aunt looking directly at him, her face full of questions.

"Tell me, Stevie, what did you learn today?"

He was quiet for just a moment, trying to process what he had discovered about himself, but also not wanting to sound stupid or lame. After all, trying to tell someone that the wind responded to your thoughts and that you received a warning from…well…somewhere, was not easy.

"Well, you were right about the wind. It did seem to pick up when I thought it might. And I saw something in the light. Aunt Bessie, but I'm not sure what it was."

"Come on, let's walk," his aunt said, as they took the meandering path back to the Walnut Grove reserve.

"The wind did respond to your command, Stevie," she said, as they walked. "You are able to communicate with the elements. That's one of the reasons you enjoy skateboarding so much, because you are close to the air, and are often carried, or propelled on a breeze. Although you may not have realized it, you have been communicating with the elements, particularly the wind, most of your life. What I need you to remember is that the wind will answer your call when you need it most. Imagine it, and make it so."

"And the warning in the light?" Stevie asked, still puzzled by its meaning.

"Well, firstly, when you need additional protection, encircle yourself with the light and energy of the sun. When you do this – when you step outside negative thoughts and influences – you are able to see fragments of the future, Stevie. What you saw today, was one possibility. Only you can determine whether to act on that information at the time. Our visions of the future are not always accurate and are indicators only. But I would say this, if you are in a situation where you have misgivings of any sort, you need to listen to your instincts."

They had almost reached the car.

"There is one more thing, Aunt Bessie."

"Yes, Stevie, what is worrying you?"

"You know already. It's Jem."

Aunt Bessie unlocked the car doors.

"Yes, Stevie, I know what is happening to Jem, but at this point there is not much you can do. But I can do one thing, and that is protect him with light. I will be giving him an Illuminator stone in a new watch I'm giving him for his birthday. It will, at least for the moment, stop him becoming a Greycaster."

"And the Hoods?" Stevie asked.

"Leave them to me," Aunt Bessie said.

Chapter 11

A Skating Challenge

The days passed uneventfully for Stevie and, with Aunt Bessie's reassuring presence, the Vegas household went about its business with a sense of normality, despite the looming threats around them. Aunt Bessie was true to her word in handling the Hoods. She had encircled the home with the most powerful spell she could conjure – a brilliant, invisible sheath of pure white light, drawn from the sun. Only Illuminators could see the defense, which pulsated with positive energy and warned off any negative, dark penetrations. This circle of light affected Jem the most. He was no longer drawn so much to the computer and the dark games Devlin Hood was teaching him on Vision Quest. He spent more time with the family, coming downstairs just to sit and talk whenever they were gathered in a group. His face brightened, the dark circles under his eyes disappeared and, for the first time in a long time, he looked at Stevie through brotherly eyes with very little of the resentment that had clouded his thoughts in the past months.

Stevie did all he could to strengthen the foundations of their relationship, going back to their old habits of playing backyard soccer after school, while his parents involved him again in caring for the animals in their vet practice. One particular dog, a golden Retriever cross Jem named Fluffy because of his shaggy coat, almost became a family pet. Sylvia Vegas was caring for him after a neighbor had brought him over to her practice late one afternoon. He had been clipped by a car and they could find no collar or microchip. It appeared Fluffy was a stray, but as was the rule in the Vegas household, the strays were always given to good homes.

Fluffy and Jem hit it off instantly though and Jem was

DAWN OF THE SHADOWCASTERS

working on his mum and dad, subtly trying to bend the rules.

"You know, Mum, it's good having Fluffy about. Did you see him chasing the soccer ball yesterday with Stevie and me? He fits right in, doesn't he?"

His mum had to admit that Fluffy was a distraction for Jem, from the unending hours he was spending in his room. Stevie could see the glances his parents exchanged and, when Stevie and Jem had left the room, he heard the whispering that maybe, under the circumstances, they could bend the rules just this once.

Their previous dog had died soon after they returned from Smithson and enough time had elapsed now to consider a new family pet. Fluffy seemed to come along at just the right time and between Stevie's focus on Jem and Fluffy's liking for Jem, there were good reasons to consider making Fluffy a permanent member of the household.

"I'll check with the pound again to see that no one has claimed him," his mum said to Jem as they were walking out the door to school. "I'm not promising anything, mind you," she added.

"Really," Jem said. "You'd do that? Stevie did you hear that, Fluffy might just be able to stay."

Stevie grinned at his brother. "And then there'll be no excuses to stay in your room and play the computer all afternoon."

"Actually," Sylvia said, "there will be conditions if Fluffy stays. Jem he'll be your dog and you will need to look after him – feed him and play with him of an afternoon. What do you say?"

Jem didn't hesitate. "OK, Mum, I hear you. No computer of an afternoon if Fluffy comes to live with us."

"You got it," she said, ruffling his hair as the two Vegas boys gathered their backpacks and sneaked a last piece of toast to take to school.

They took the short route to school, and Stevie decided not to take his skateboard, opting instead to walk beside Jem. They were nearly to the school gates when they saw Devlin Hood. Feeling his presence long before Devlin Hood caught up with them, Stevie immediately encircled both himself and Jem with the white light he had learned about in Walnut Grove.

Hood was temporarily caught off guard and Stevie sensed the puzzlement at first, which quickly turned to anger. But there was nothing Devlin could do to shake the cloak of protection Stevie had so strongly caste about himself and Jem.

Devlin kept his distance.

"Hey, Jem, missed you this morning. I thought we were walking to school today?"

"Ahh...I decided to walk to school with Stevie," Jem answered, trying not to meet Devlin's hard stare.

Stevie fought the anger down that was threatening to engulf him. How dare Devlin Hood try to come between them, but he knew that confronting Devlin now would be a mistake. His instincts told him not to push Jem too much; they were only just starting to get along well and he knew Jem wasn't quite ready to choose between him and a very persuasive, manipulative Devlin Hood. Instead, Stevie kept his cool.

"What do you want, Hood?" he said evenly.

Devlin Hood fixed his dark eyes on Stevie. "What's it to you, Vegas? I've got business with Jem, not you."

"Well actually you don't. Jem and I are late for class."

But Devlin Hood was not going to give up easily. "What do you say, Jem? Want to walk to class with me?"

Jem looked first at his brother and then at Devlin Hood, not knowing what to do. He didn't want to upset Stevie, but at the same time he wanted to keep his friendship with Devlin.

"I...ahh...yeah, sure, Devlin."

Stevie felt the anger rise again, but knew that it was useless to create a scene in front of Jem. Instead, he said simply, "It's OK, Jem, you go with Devlin. I've got to catch up with some other friends."

"You sure, Stevie?" Jem said.

"Yeah, sure. I'll catch you up after school. Maybe we can walk home together?"

"Yeah, maybe, Stevie. I'll catch you."

Stevie gave Devlin Hood one last glare.

"You might want to check the noticeboard, Vegas, on your way to class." Hood said as Stevie was about to walk off. "There's a skate comp down at the skatepark on Friday night. Don't know about you, but I'll be there. You might want to check out my 900...been practicing it for the past month. You're not the only skateboarder in town, you know."

"Is that a challenge, Hood?"

"Up to you, that's if you're not afraid of losing?" the boy replied.

Stevie gave him his full attention then, noticing as he did that Devlin Hood's aura was turning a darker shade of black with every passing minute, he walked within inches of him, looking him directly in the eyes. He was not afraid.

"You don't want to mess with me, Hood," he said, projecting his energy outwards and, at the same time, imagining the wind picking up. Within minutes, as if answering his call, the light breeze of that morning became stronger.

Devlin Hood laughed. "Tricks and games, Vegas. I know what you're trying to do and quite frankly, it's lame. Let's finish this at the skatepark."

But Stevie held his gaze. He was not backing down, and particularly not in front of Jem.

"It's you who needs to sharpen up your act. I'll meet you at the skatepark, or anywhere for that matter. Game on."

Hood turned away then. "Come on, Jem, let's get out of here. Your brother's just boring me now."

They went to move off, but Stevie wanted the last say.

"Jem, I'll see you tonight. Hood, don't forget to take your science book to class."

Hood turned back, a little puzzled by Stevie's parting shot but, as he did, the wind that was swirling around them became stronger and the science book Devlin had been carrying simply blew out of his hands and into the air.

Stevie turned away then, but not before he caught the glimpse of Devlin Hood chasing after the pages of his science book, hundreds of which were now blowing across the schoolyard.

Chapter 12

Illumination

Sure enough, when Stevie checked the noticeboard the local skating association was advertising a mega skating comp on Friday night. It was the usual rules and Stevie had competed in the open class before, along with other elite skaters he knew and trained with. What was different this time was Devlin Hood had entered and this caused Stevie a decent amount of soul searching. Added to Devlin's obvious Shadowcaster powers was his mention of a 900 aerial trick. It wasn't until later that afternoon at school that Stevie remembered his premonition – a warning against performing the 900. Like every other skater that competed, Stevie would be forced to match trick for trick and, if a competitor successfully completed the 900, he would have to try it…and beat it.

The days at school flew by that week but Stevie was restless. At the back of his mind was the looming skate comp, and the ever present knowledge that the Barrons were most likely in Valley Dale. Only Aunt Bessie's presence at the Vegas home reassured him. When she was around, it was as if his fear of the Shadowcasters was gone. He knew that as long as he was in her protection even Barron and his followers could not touch him.

It had become habit for Stevie and Aunt Bessie to walk during the evenings, after dinner, when the cool of the summer evening had permeated Valley Dale's hot pavements, sprinklers were turned on, and the neighborhood relaxed after the heat of the day. The trees, particularly, responded to the evening's cool air and Stevie always noticed the ever so slight breeze that rippled through their leaves. Since that day in Walnut Grove, Stevie's attention was always on the wind. He knew its secret, that with intention and focus, it would respond to his thoughts.

The night before the skating comp, he walked with Aunt Bessie along the meandering path that ran adjacent to Valley Dale's river. He could smell the nearby ocean and he thought that maybe a storm was approaching.

"You understand now the power of nature," his aunt said, interrupting his thoughts. "And how when we become one with it, tune into it, we can harness its energy."

He let his concentration on the elements fade for a moment. As usual Aunt Bessie had that knowing look on her face, and he marveled yet again at just how wise she really was.

"I think so, Aunt Bessie. I don't really know, but I have seen things with you, like the way the wind responds to my thoughts that makes me think there's a lot we don't know."

"Precisely, Stevie. But the real gift, the real talent, is in believing that it's possible," she said.

Stevie took the thought in, immediately knowing somewhere deep inside that belief and intention were the keys to entering nature's world.

"I understand," he said.

As if reading his thoughts, his aunt said, "There's something else bothering you?"

Not for the first time, Stevie was glad his aunt could read his mind.

"Yes there is, Aunt Bessie. I need to know more about Illuminators. How'd we get to be this way? How long have Illuminators been doing this…fighting the Shadowcasters and what gives the Illuminator stones their power?"

His aunt sat down on the cool grass by the river and motioned for him to do the same. All around the sounds of the nearby running water blended with the call of the cicadas and the ever present rustling of the breeze.

"I'm glad you want to know, Stevie," she said. "It's time for you to find out more about your birthright, and about our past."

He settled into the cool green of the grass.

"There have always been Illuminators and, of course, there have always been Shadowcasters. The earliest Illuminators were those that stood against injustice, but they suffered great pain and loss as a result. The world is not always a fair place, Stevie, and just because you stand against power, corruption, greed and manipulation for self-gain, doesn't mean you will live a charmed life. In many cases those that stood against evil in those early days often died too young, in poverty and without influence or position. Shadowcasters though, who held the power in the world, would simply destroy an Illuminator either through curses, destroying their reputations or making sure enough people shunned and avoided them. It was only then, when our lives were at their darkest, lowest point that we were forced to think outside ourselves and begin to discover the source of our true power as Illuminators. We began to discover that nature was the real Illuminator – that it held more power than all the Shadowcasters together. In our suffering, we embraced nature's healing gifts and it was there that we discovered the Illuminator stones, and how we could use the elements – earth, wind and water."

Stevie let the cool evening breeze embrace him. He wanted to hear more. "Go on, Aunt Bessie. What happened then and how'd you get to be an Illuminator?"

"Questions. A searching mind is always seeking questions, but sometimes the answers will come without force, Stevie. I can tell you about our history, but there are certain things…powers, you must discover for yourself – the ultimate awareness for an Illuminator to reach is Luminous…but you are not ready for that yet," she said quickly.

"Luminous, Aunt Bessie…?"

But Aunt Bessie was impatient to finish her story. "As I said there are some things you must discover for yourself. Now, back to our story… As you know the Illuminator stones are the purest white quartz, honed over time by the wind, air and water. These stones carry memories of past times, and so it is with each Illuminator stone – gathered from sacred sites and destined for each individual Illuminator. The stone I gave you, Stevie, needs to be awakened…by you. This stone has memories of past times…and battles and when its owner – you – are at your most powerful, your stone will respond in kind. So we Illuminators gathered our stones, and we began to communicate with nature. This mind telepathy if you like, was the foundation of our ability to read human minds. With each new discovery, Illuminators grew more powerful. The more we used our minds to communicate with nature and each other, the more open we became to receiving messages and premonitions through time dimensions."

"And the Shadowcasters? What were they doing?"

Aunt Bessie picked up a nearby stone, dark in color, and threw it into the water. "Well, unfortunately, they too began to develop their powers. They sought out and found the blackest of stones, the onyx, and cast spells and curses into these stones. They had learned to read minds early in our history, which always gave them an edge when it came to gathering followers and placing themselves in positions of money and power in society. While I don't know the extent of their spell casting, I do know they have been harnessing the power of the sun too, but not to create light. They have been experimenting with and creating the energy that fuels fire and they use this combined with curses, to trap and destroy Illuminators. We need to be very careful, Stevie, very careful not to be caught by the Shadowcasters. Where there are more than three, their power is stronger. We must avoid, at all costs, a confrontation with more than three Shadowcasters."

"But, Aunt Bessie, surely you have a way of preventing this from happening?" Stevie said, not for a moment thinking there was nothing his aunt couldn't do.

"Maybe, Stevie. I don't honestly know. I have been experimenting with the air or more particularly, the rain clouds but I haven't been able to master it yet. I think that we need more than one Illuminator to accomplish this, which is why I have been teaching you to communicate with nature. If perhaps you and another…"

"The power of three or more you mean," Stevie said.

"Yes, I think it would take you and me, perhaps Mary Lou…or another."

Stevie jumped up then. "There is another? One of us?"

His aunt got up too, placing her hand on Stevie to steady herself.

"I didn't want to tell you, not yet but I think we will need her before the end… Yes, Stevie, it's your mother."

Stevie jumped then in surprise. "My mum. You're kidding me? Mum…an Illuminator?"

"Of course, Stevie, but she doesn't know it yet and I want you to keep it a secret. Remember your reaction when you found out, well Sylvia…your mum…has not been prepared. It will be a shock for her."

Stevie nodded. "I know. Of course, but how will we tell her."

Aunt Bessie smiled. "When the time comes, Stevie, we will not have to. She will know."

Chapter 13

Game On

Stevie put on his favorite jeans and sleeveless T-shirt for the skate comp. Already there was interest in the competition amongst his friends. Mary Lou had promised to come and watch him, and Bren Lee was going. He would help Stevie prepare. Devlin Hood had asked Jem to accompany him and Stevie had not protested. He had enough to worry about and he knew arguing with Jem would just push him further away.

Aunt Bessie would also come, with his mum and dad. He felt comforted by that. For days he had been searching for a way out of performing the 900, but it was useless. If another competitor performed it, he would have to do better but the premonition there was danger in the 900, was uppermost in his mind.

As he put on his wristband and reached for his competition skateboard, he instinctively touched his Illuminator stone and uttered a silent prayer. "Please, God, or whatever you are, show me a way to beat Devlin Hood." It was at that moment Stevie got a mental image of the wind. He knew somehow it was the key. Grabbing his gear he made his way down the stairs, two at a time.

"Mum, Mum, are you ready? We've got to go."

Sylvia Vegas appeared from behind the kitchen door.

"OK, Stevie, keep that shirt of yours on. Let's get you there then."

The drive to the skatepark was as quick as his mum dared to go. Stevie noticed that she seemed just as nervous as he felt. Only Aunt Bessie remained relatively calm.

"Remember, Stevie, let go of doubt and trust your mind's voice."

Stevie nodded in the darkness. "I'll try," was all he could

manage.

When they got to the skatepark the crowds were gathering. On one side of the huge ramps Valley Dale had installed only last year, was Devlin Hood's camp. Stevie could just make out Jem's face in the crowd. He smiled and waved to him, determined not to be rattled by Devlin's games. He noticed Mary Lou's father there too. Shadowcasters, he thought to himself, and where were the Barrons? That would have made the picture complete, he thought, with a sinking feeling. He was just about to give into certain defeat, even before the competition had started, when he caught sight of Mary Lou and Bren Lee. He hurried over to them, eager to be amongst friends.

"Hi, Stevie. Are you ready for the skate?" Bren Lee asked, searching Stevie's face for any telltale signs of fear. Bren Lee knew that Devlin Hood and his followers needed this victory tonight, to unseat Stevie's confidence…and fear always led to a downward spiral in confidence.

"I'm fine…you know, a little nervous but that's the way it is before a big comp."

He turned to Mary Lou. In the gathering shadows he noticed she had on a sky blue skirt and white T-shirt.

"Hey, what gives? Where's the leathers?" He laughed, despite himself.

With a mock twirl, she said, "It's all for you, Stevie Vegas. I could hardly come in my motorbike leathers could I…'specially when I'm taking you for ice cream after the big comp. I just had to be dressed nice to accompany the winner."

Stevie shook his head, his confidence low.

"I wouldn't bet on me," he said.

Bren Lee placed a firm hand on his arm.

"Would you mind, Mary Lou, if Stevie and I did a bit of pre-skating preparation?"

She smiled a sunny smile, as if hoping to lift Stevie's spirits, which were clearly flagging.

"No problem. I've just caught sight of Aunt Bessie and your mum, Stevie. I'll go and get them seated."

With that she was off, her blue skirt swirling in the gentle breeze that had sprung up.

Bren Lee turned back to Stevie.

"You need to find that calm place within, Stevie. The space that allows you to be truly who you are."

"Oh, come on, Bren Lee. Not now," Stevie said. "I appreciate it, but I just can't focus now."

"Precisely. That's the point. Now look into my eyes."

Stevie shifted impatiently from foot to foot. He didn't want to appear ungrateful…

"Stevie," Bren Lee said, "look at me."

Knowing there was no way out of it, Stevie obliged.

"Now, look into my eyes and concentrate on my voice. Take three deep breaths, Stevie, and imagine yourself in the middle of the forest. You can hear the ocean and feel the wind on your cheek, on your arms and legs."

Stevie concentrated and took himself back to Walnut Grove, where Aunt Bessie had taught him about the power of the wind. Despite himself, he drifted further and further into his imagi-nation, forgetting for a moment he was in the middle of the skatepark.

"The wind is getting stronger, lifting you up and taking you with it. You don't fight this wind, Stevie, you go with it and you become one with it. It takes you over the mountains and over the ocean…"

Stevie felt the wind and rode with it, as if on a waterless wave. He imagined himself on his stakeboard, riding the wind. Below him the ocean stretched out like a vast reservoir teeming with life. The mountains loomed to his right and he turned his board to them, shifting into the currents, dipping and twirling. Bren Lee's voice continued but now it was now a small voice inside him, far off and fading. He only felt the wind and heard the sounds of the air currents around him. He was the wind.

"Coming back to consciousness…slowly…calmly…surely…"

He was interrupted by Bren Lee's voice again.

"I'm going to count from five to one and you will awaken. Five, you are feeling relaxed. Four, you are awakening now. Three, coming back into your present surroundings. Two, feeling relaxed and ready for anything. One, wide awake."

Stevie opened his eyes to see Bren Lee's face, intense and passionate.

"How are you, Stevie? Feeling better?"

"Ahh…I guess." He shook his arms. "Yeah, actually I'm feeling pretty good."

Bren Lee smiled. "Good. And how are your confidence levels?"

Stevie grinned, and winked at Bren Lee. "Well if I can ride my board tonight like I rode the wind just then, I'm set, aren't I."

"Imagine if, Stevie. That is the key. Imagine you are catching the wind tonight. It's on our side you know."

Stevie nodded, just as Aunt Bessie and Sylvia Vegas appeared with Mary Lou.

"It's time," his mum said. "They've just called your name."

Kissing him gently on the forehead, Sylvie Vegas whispered, "Be careful, Stevie."

Mary Lou gave him her brightest smile. And Bren Lee looked directly at him with confidence. Only Aunt Bessie held back, a look of concern creasing her brow.

"Remember your instincts, Stevie," Aunt Bessie said. "When all else fails, trust your inner voice because it will be your guide."

And then, silently, Aunt Bessie projected her thoughts. "Something is wrong tonight, Stevie. I don't know what it is yet, but I will find out. In the meantime, be careful and remember you have many friends with you."

Stevie nodded to her, and smiled at them confidently.

"I'll be all right. You'll see."

And with that he was off to the marshaling area.

When he arrived, he felt Devlin Hood's presence. Unmistakable. The dark shadows were around him, darting and weaving like a deathly aura. He reached for his necklace and imagined the sun's rays energizing it, energizing him. But Devlin Hood could see the white light growing brighter around Stevie.

"Hey, Vegas, you ready for the 900?" Hood said, throwing out the challenge and wanting to dent Stevie's growing confidence.

"We'll see," Stevie replied. He didn't want to appear over confident, and certainly didn't want to give anything away to Devlin Hood.

The draw was finally announced and, although he knew it before it was read out, Stevie would face Devlin Hood in the competition.

He glanced over in the semi-darkness. Hood was smiling at him.

"Helps when you have friends in high places, Vegas," Devlin Hood whispered.

"Always on the attack aren't you, Devlin. Maybe you should think about what is behind you."

Devlin Hood spun around quickly, only to find thin air.

"That's it, Hood, you never know what's behind you," Stevie said.

Hood turned to face him. His eyes narrowed. "It's you, Vegas, who needs to watch your back. You just never know when you'll meet up with old enemies."

"What do you mean by that, Hood? Any funny stuff...I won't take lying down."

At that moment, the marshal called their names out. They were to take their places on Ramp 1 and wait for the starter signal.

Stevie let his concentration on Devlin Hood go, making his way up the steep climb to the top of the ramp. Below, he could make out his family and friends. He could feel their support. On the other side of the ramp Devlin Hood stood triumphantly, waving to the crowd. He was to go first and dropped in with surprising agility. Stevie thought, for the first time that night, that here was a competitor who might match his own skill.

He watched while Devlin Hood skated deftly from side to side, building up speed in an effort to get enough air for his trick. Back and forth he went, the crowd cheering him on. When his speed and timing were right he began his 900. Stevie watched him, as if in slow motion. He turned first one, then two, and then three summersaults. The crowd went wild. This was the first time they'd seen a 900, and only the best pulled them off.

Stevie waited for the cheers to die down. He glanced below, searching for his Aunt Bessie in the crowd. What he needed now was a miracle. He wasn't entirely sure he could pull this off. He took a few deep breaths and stilled his mind, listening for its guidance. A small voice answered his searching. He didn't know whether it was instinct or a gut feeling, but he felt sure he shouldn't attempt the 900. But he had to, or risk being shown up by Devlin Hood – a Shadowcaster.

He gritted his teeth and concentrated on the breeze that had sprung up around him. He remembered the wind and the way he was propelled effortlessly over the ocean and over the mountains. Surely, it would be his friend tonight. He murmured silently to the breeze. "Give me your air, help me."

He dropped in effortlessly and skated from side to side of the ramp, building speed. When he was ready to perform the 900, he held off. He wasn't sure he had enough speed or air. Better to be sure. He concentrated on being ready. Back and forth he went, faster and faster. When he could no longer delay, he propelled his board skywards. Round and round, the only thing in his mind was a single question: did he have enough height and speed for a third turn? As he was about to execute it, something came into his mind. In a split second he saw Jacob Barron's face. Close and full of hate. The force of the vision interrupted his concentration and at the last moment, he pulled off a half turn trying to steady himself from the fall that was almost a certainty. Using all his skill he tried to hit the ramp upright with his board but it wasn't enough. At lightning speed and with the weight of the g-force pulling him down, he lost his footing and went skidding down the ramp, his board hurtling in front of him. As he slid, he felt a bone break in his wrist with a sickening crack. He slid the rest of the way downward, winded and groggy, and lay nursing his wrist.

Within minutes the marshals were with him and, checking for neck and back injuries, called for a stretcher. The last thing he remembered was a cheering Devlin Hood from above on the ramp's ledge. And something else. In the shadows of the crowd he thought he saw a face he knew. Jacob Barron.

Chapter 14

An Emergency Meeting

Stevie woke to the bright lights of a hospital room in Valley Dale. His mum's worried face hovered over him, and Aunt Bessie stood behind her, her face full of worry.

"Oh, thank God, Stevie, you're awake. How are you feeling?" his mum said.

"Umm…OK, Mum. I'm OK," he replied. He wanted to be strong for her, despite the throbbing pain in his head.

"Son, you'll will need your wrist set. It's broken. You also have a concussion," his mum said.

Stevie tried to sit up using his good hand to lift himself off the pillows, but the pain in head forced him back down.

"My head hurts…"

"Don't try to move, Stevie, not yet. You've sustained a heavy knock to your head – the x-rays are OK, but you've got to rest."

Stevie smiled weakly. "Well, that's good news. Aunt Bessie?

Aunt Bessie stepped forward, patting his hand and smiling kindly at her nephew.

"You gave us quite a scare, Stevie, but we are lucky. It could have been worse. A lot worse."

Despite the fog that seemed to encompass his brain, he opened his mind to Aunt Bessie. He could sense she was holding something back.

"Yes, that's right, Stevie. It could have been worse. Devlin Hood set a trap for you. He planned this whole thing. You were never meant to complete your 900 turn."

Stevie looked directly at her then, trying to hide the surprise in his face. "And Jacob Barron? I thought I saw him in the crowd."

"You did, Stevie. Devlin Hood used his Shadowcaster powers, combining with Jacob Barron's to make you doubt yourself.

That's why you hesitated. That's why you fell. When you doubt you lose faith in your instincts; you set yourself up for failure."

His mum interrupted their thought communication.

"What is it, you two? There's no need to worry anymore. Stevie's fine. Stop looking so serious. I think that's enough for now. Stevie, we'll be back in the morning."

She kissed him goodbye.

"And Mary Lou, Jem and Bren Lee?" Stevie said.

"They're outside keeping a vigil. But no visitors tonight, young man. We'll drop them home and they can visit you when they release you home tomorrow. With a bit of luck you'll be discharged in the morning. Your dad's at home worried sick. We better get home and put his mind to rest."

She leaned over and kissed Stevie softly on the cheek.

Aunt Bessie did the same, but projected one last thought. "When you get out tomorrow I want us all to meet. We need a plan."

Stevie nodded, speaking so his mum could hear. "Yes, Aunt Bessie, I'll see you in the morning. I want to talk to Bren Lee too. I need to go over why I failed, despite everything I tried."

"Enough for tonight, Stevie. We'll see you tomorrow."

Stevie waved them off. Alone in the room, he suddenly felt very vulnerable. The pain in his temples began to ease thanks to the painkillers the nurse had given him half an hour before. His wrist had been immobilized with a cast. Skateboarding was off the agenda for at least two months.

He let his thoughts take over in the quietness of the hospital room. How could he have fallen? He never fell, and yet, looking back on it, it seemed inevitable that he would not make the 900. If only he had listened to the warning he had received that day in Walnut Grove but, he reasoned, he had no way of knowing Devlin Hood would set him up. He had performed the 900 before in practice sessions with his coach. He should have been able to make the final turn.

He ran through the events of that night. When he fell and was lying at the bottom of the ramp, he remembered Jacob Barron's face in the crowd. It couldn't have been. Jacob was in a coma after his fall during their skateboarding duel in Smithson. The doctors said it was unlikely he would recover, but Aunt Bessie seemed certain he had helped Devlin Hood in his mind attack at the skatepark. Stevie thought back over the past year since Smithson. The Shadowcasters had systematically built up their numbers in Valley Dale, paving the way for the Barrons to come. But how had Jacob Barron recovered?

Stevie remembered the voices he had heard in his mind – Jacob Barron had been making a deal with someone. He thought hard. He needed to talk to his Aunt Bessie again. What power on this earth could heal a boy in a coma? He remembered the cursed stones of the Shadowcasters. He had stolen one of the Barrons' cursed stones and destroyed it, sending it down to the bottom of the Katounga River, but there had been two cursed stones and the second was still in the Barrons' possession. Could it have brought Jacob out of his coma? Anything was possible. There was much he had to learn about the power of Shadowcasters, and much he had to learn about Illuminators…about himself.

The pain in his head returned, just as the night nurse entered with a sleeping tablet for him.

"Take this, young man, and I guarantee you'll sleep well tonight," the nurse said.

Stevie obliged, eager for dreamless sleep. As he drifted off, images of giant skate ramps filled his mind and he was falling…falling into a black, bottomless pit where not the faintest of light penetrated. Despite what the nurse had told him, he slept fitfully, waiting for the dawn.

Morning did come, even though Stevie doubted it during the long night. His mum and Aunt Bessie arrived to pick him up and he was discharged with a stern warning from the doctor to stay off his skateboard for two months.

As they drove home, Stevie wondered what was next in his life. With the arrival of the Barrons it seemed obvious to him that he would one day have to face Jacob Barron again...and Devlin Hood.

When they pulled up outside the Vegas home, Mary Lou and Bren Lee were waiting at the front door, eager to see Stevie and make sure he was all right.

As he greeted them, he sensed Mary Lou had something on her mind. Bren Lee's features were intense, even for him. Jem was nowhere to be seen. He had gone to school that morning and would be home later. As they ushered him into the lounge room where a pillow and blanket lay waiting, on the Vegas' most comfortable couch, it was obvious they all wanted to speak about what had happened at the skatepark. His mum hovered around him, fussing and wanting to wait on his every need.

"Mum, stop it. I mean it. Really I'm OK," he said, his tone slightly impatient with the fussing.

"All right, Stevie. I understand you want to catch up with your friends but I'm just worried about you, you know? It was a heavy fall you took last night," she said, mentally running through her checklist, used to nursing two sons since babyhood. Color good. Clear eyes. No signs of temperature or pain.

"You know what?" Stevie said.

"Umm. No. I'm not a mind reader," his mum said, laughing at her son.

"I would love beef stroganoff for dinner tonight," Stevie said. "With fettuccine too."

"Really," his mum said, with a smile. It was Stevie's favorite and an appetite was a good sign he was recovering from the concussion. "But I'll need to run down to the shops for the ingredients. Aunt Bessie can you keep an eye on our patient?"

Aunt Bessie nodded.

"It's OK, darling. You go. Stevie will be safe with me."

As she pulled out of the drive, Aunt Bessie closed the

connecting door to the lounge room.

"I'm glad you are all here. We have a lot we need to discuss – not the least is Jacob Barron's presence in Valley Dale. Mary Lou, I understand you have something to tell us," she said.

Stevie looked across at Mary Lou. She was dressed casually in jeans and a T-shirt, but she looked far from comfortable. He sensed her thoughts were urgent.

"What is it, Mary Lou?" he asked, gently.

She looked over at him, as though she was going to cry. "Oh, Stevie, I'm so sorry."

He didn't understand. "Sorry? Mary Lou, you have nothing to be sorry about."

She put her head in her hands. "Oh, but I do, Stevie. I stood by and did nothing. I couldn't do anything, there were too many."

"What do you mean, Mary Lou? You're not making sense."

Aunt Bessie interrupted. "Mary Lou, calm down and tell us your story. Take your time. You are amongst friends."

Mary Lou sat back in her chair and took a deep breath.

"OK. When I got home from the hospital last night, I noticed the light on in our front sitting room and muffled voices coming from inside. It was unusual because my dad doesn't have visitors after about 8 pm. Nobody heard me come in, so I sneaked back outside to the front window to take a better look…"

"And?" Stevie said, sitting forward, eager for the story to continue.

"There were a lot of people in the room…Devlin Hood and his father, another man I didn't know and a woman. There was also a boy there, Stevie, about your age with the darkest of eyes. Stevie, they called him by name. Jacob Barron."

The room began to spin for Stevie. It couldn't be, but yet it had to be. Aunt Bessie moved quickly over to the couch, putting a calming hand on his shoulder. Immediately the room's spin stopped.

Bren Lee, who had been sitting quietly in the corner of the

room, got up and sat in the chair next to Mary Lou.

"The news you have brought us is important. We knew the Barrons had moved back to Valley Dale but, so far, no one has seen either Jacob or his father, Chris. We now know they are here. Did you hear anything, Mary Lou?"

"It's not so much what I heard, Bren Lee, but what they were thinking."

"Go ahead," Aunt Bessie said.

Mary Lou looked straight at Stevie. "I…ah…Jacob and Devlin were mind reading each other and Jacob was congratulating him on a job well done. I'm sorry, Stevie, you were set up. And that's not the worst of it. They are using a cursed stone to manipulate things, and to recruit more followers. They are trying to recruit Jem. I didn't do anything, Stevie. I'm sorry, I should have done something then, projected my thoughts, tried to talk to my dad…"

"No, Mary Lou. There was nothing you could do. But bringing us this information is important. Cursed stone. Aunt Bessie, what does this mean?" Stevie said. He was horrified at the thought that the stone may be used to turn Jem against him.

Aunt Bessie was silent for a few moments, deep in thought. She looked at each one of them in turn – at Stevie's anxious face, at Mary Lou whose guilt and worry was so evident and at Bren Lee who, as always, was sitting calmly but intensely on his chair.

"Firstly, Mary Lou, I don't want you confronting your father over anything. Do you understand? You are helping us best by bringing us this information. And I don't want you putting yourself in danger. Secondly, our priority is Jem. We must do all we can to get him away from Devlin Hood's influence. Next, I don't want you, Stevie, to worry. We Illuminators have our own special stones to counteract the cursed stones. We are not without our means. Bren Lee, I will need you to leave Valley Dale on business for me…there is someone I need you to visit. Something I need you to get."

Bren Lee nodded. "Anything, Aunt Bessie. I can leave today if needed."

"Yes…yes, Bren, I think that will be wise…as soon as possible."

Aunt Bessie continued, "Stevie, it is time to talk to your mother…tell her everything. We need her to accept her Illuminator powers. The more Illuminators we have in this house, the less danger Jem will be in."

"But, Aunt Bessie…the cursed stone. I've seen their power. What can we do about it…break into the Barron estate again and steal it." He said this with more than a hint of sarcasm in his voice.

She laughed then, merriment twinkling in her eyes. "I know you can't use your skateboard for a few months but I'm sure there are other ways of getting over the Barron estate wall."

"Aunt Bessie, seriously, there is no way we can get into that estate. First time we stole Chris Barron's stone…we were lucky…second time…well let's just say a second attempt is suicidal. What are we going to do? Just walk through those gates?"

Aunt Bessie got up, full of confidence it appeared, and began pacing the floor, deep in thought.

"Maybe. Just maybe, we can walk through the gates without being seen."

Had Aunt Bessie taken leave of her senses? Walk through the gates?

"Tea, anybody?" Aunt Bessie said, calmly.

Chapter 15

A Secret Revealed

Stevie recovered his strength as the days wore on. His wrist was less and less tender, and his energy began to return as his concussion healed. Aunt Bessie kept a watchful eye on Jem, even going as far as creating an amulet in the guise of a watch to wear on his wrist. She told him it was simply a family heirloom and Jem, obligingly, wore it.

His dad came and went from work, fussing over him just as his mum did. He was anxious to be back on his feet though. Bren Lee had mysteriously left town on Aunt Bessie's orders and Mary Lou brought new information on the Shadowcasters, she had obtained from listening at doorways, and looking through windows. Although she put herself in danger of discovery, she had never once thought about not helping Stevie.

Through the long days of his recovery, she was often by his side – whether it was sitting by his side trying to cheer him up, or projecting her thoughts that everything would be OK.

But would it? Not once during the long days of recovery did Stevie think for one minute that the Vegas family were out of danger. He could feel it everywhere – on the wind and in the vague gut feeling that something was coming, and it wasn't something good. True to her word, Aunt Bessie had arranged for him and his mum to take a drive to the river with her…to get Stevie out of the house, if only for a while.

They packed a picnic afternoon tea full of the foods he liked. There were rolls stuffed with Italian meats, an assortment of vintage cheeses – his favorites – olives of course and a chocolate cake to finish, all washed down by lemon sodas.

As they drove past the suburbia of Valley Dale's outer rim, Stevie wondered whether they were doing the right thing – this afternoon's drive had been engineered by Aunt Bessie so they could tell his mum she was an Illuminator, and the seriousness of the Shadowcaster threat they were under. Hopefully, it would not shock or worry her too much. He wondered and worried. His mum had always been so conservative. As the town's vet, and a busy mum with two young boys, she had gone about her business quietly and competently. She was known as someone the townspeople could rely on – the vet who took the time to come out after hours if there was an emergency, rain, hail or shine. She helped out at the school canteen when she could. In short, Sylvia Vegas was an exceptional wife, mother and Valley Dale citizen. It wasn't until Smithson, when Jem had been injured and Jacob Barron had taken such a bad fall at the skate park, that trouble had entered her normally predictable life.

Stevie could see his mum was preoccupied with her own thoughts too. He knew she wondered why Aunt Bessie had insisted they go for a picnic, especially when everyone knew how busy she was with a vet hospital full of sick animals but odd things always had a way of happening when Aunt Bessie was around, Stevie conceded and his mum would be used to that by now.

His mum had told him that growing up her family had always considered Aunt Bessie 'eccentric,' and that odd coincidences had always accompanied her visits. When his mum was a girl she would be thinking about needing something, and when her aunt visited that very thing was given to her as a present. Stevie knew that his mum and her family had stopped asking Aunt Bessie how she 'knew' because she always replied, "I just know, that's all."

Both Stevie and his mum were still deep in thought as the car pulled into the picnic area. Stevie offered to carry the picnic basket, but his mum told him he would do no such thing with a broken wrist. Instead he carried the fold up chairs under his good arm.

They picked the grassiest spot, out of the way of the general park traffic – a spot close to the river and Stevie marveled, yet again, at the peacefulness. He sat and listened to the gentle sound of the water, while his mother got out the thickly sliced sourdough sandwiches and rolls she'd made that morning jammed full of a selection of meats, crispy lettuce and freshly picked tomatoes from the Vegas garden. His aunt poured three glasses of her homemade lemon soda, and Stevie couldn't help but think how normal it was – sitting eating sandwiches by the banks of the river. His aunt interrupted his thoughts.

"Isn't this lovely, Sylvia?" she said. "It reminds me of the time when you were a young girl and we took a picnic down to the river near your parent's farm. You were only about six or seven, if I recall."

Sylvia nodded. "Why, Aunt Bessie, that was such a long time ago. I can hardly remember it. I do remember the wonderful chicken salad you made. Oh, and those fresh apples we picked from the orchard…"

"Do you remember, Sylvia, going into the water?" his Aunt said.

"Not really. I've never been one for swimming much. To be honest the water kind of scares me. It's one of the few things that do," his mum said.

Aunt Bessie got off her chair and settled herself with Stevie and his mum on the blanket, making herself comfortable.

"Sylvia would it surprise you if I told you the reason you don't like the water is because you nearly drowned that day?"

His mum looked surprised. "Drowned, what are talking about, Aunt Bessie? I don't remember that at all. We had a picnic by the river. It was a beautiful day and then there was a storm and we packed up and went home."

His aunt smiled, brushing off the breadcrumbs that had settled on Stevie's lap. "That, Sylvia, is what you want to remember. What happened…and dear, I really don't mean to frighten you at all…but there are some things that shouldn't stay hidden, is something entirely different to your memory."

Sylvia Vegas looked intently at her aunt. Stevie was all but forgotten, as she waited for her to continue. "Go on," she said, a little cautiously.

"That's very brave of you, Sylvia, because this can't be easy for you. Remember we had finished our lunch and you wanted to go for a swim. I asked you to wait half an hour until your lunch settled. I was packing up the picnic basket, thinking you had gone to pick flowers nearby, when I sensed you were in trouble. You had gone into the water and you weren't a strong swimmer in those days. The current was taking you, Sylvia, and you were in danger of drowning…"

"I…I remember blackness, Aunt Bessie…I remember a thought: that the water was closing in…I…Aunt Bessie, I was drowning wasn't I?"

His aunt reached for his mum's hand, holding it tight. "Yes, Sylvia, you were drowning but do you remember what happened next?"

"Ahh…you rescued me."

"In a way I did but in another way, you saved yourself. You see, Sylvia, I projected my thoughts to you. I reassured you and told you not to struggle against the current, but to flow with it and swim to the bank. I did this, Sylvia, through the power of my thoughts."

The afternoon had become unusually quiet, Stevie thought, while he waited for his mum's response. Even the birds had stopped singing, as if waiting for the story unfold. Sylvia Vegas sat quietly too, looking out at the river. She took her time before speaking.

"You projected your thoughts? How? That's not possible. I'm a scientist, Aunt Bessie. What do you mean?"

"Do you remember swimming for the bank?"

Sylvia nodded.

"Then think, Sylvia. Think. What made you stop fighting against the current and swim to the bank?"

His mum thought hard, wrinkling her forehead in concentration. After a moment she replied, "It was a voice, inside my head, telling me to relax, not to fight…to float and swim…I couldn't have known myself…it was…it was your voice, Aunt Bessie. It was your voice inside my head, guiding me. Reassuring me. That's how I made the bank that day. It was you, your voice."

Stevie noticed a huge smile of relief break over his mum's face, erasing the anxiety, as if she was discovering something for the first time. "You did that, Aunt Bessie? How? How on earth could your voice have got inside my head – it's just not possible."

"I did that, Sylvia, because I am an Illuminator. It's been handed down to me through our family, through the generations. I can read minds and project my thoughts. I can create a storm if I want to. Sounds crazy, I know. I had the same reaction as you, when my mother told me I was an Illuminator. You see, Sylvia, it's a family talent we have, so to speak and if I could project my thoughts to you, and you in turn heard them, what do you think that makes you?"

Sylvia's eyes widened. She looked at her Aunt Bessie first, and then her gaze rested on Stevie.

"You know, don't you?" his mum said.

Sylvia sat back, taking in everything that had passed between them that afternoon, and many, many years ago. While her scientific mind doubted, her inner knowing meant she also accepted what she was told. After a long silence, she nodded, slowly. "I am an Illuminator too?"

Aunt Bessie nodded.

"And Stevie?"

His aunt nodded again.

"Tell me then," she said. "What I need to know. Smithson…the accident with Jem. Stevie's accident. What's happening, Aunt Bessie?"

And so they told her, from the beginning. About Chris and Jacob Barron. About Illuminators and their battle with the Shadowcasters, which was as old as time itself. They told her about the Shadowcasters dark presence in Valley Dale. It wasn't until they got to Jem that she spoke.

"Jem. They want Jem," she said, panic rising in her voice.

"It's OK, Sylvia. I have protected Jem but I can't stop him seeing Devlin Hood. You must help me. We, as a family, must throw a protective psychic net around Jem to keep him safe. He is being influenced by the Shadowcasters and he is becoming what is known as a Greycaster – which is the first step towards a Shadowcaster. We have to prevent it going any further."

"Anything. Anything. But how? How can I help him?" his mum said.

"There are two things we must do. We must take away what is fuelling Jem's discontent with his family – his resentment of always being second to Stevie…whether misplaced or not, and we must break into the Barron estate in Valley Dale and steal the second cursed stone…Jacob Barron's birth stone."

"And you, Stevie?" his mum said, looking softly at her eldest. "What part are you to play in this? I won't have you injuring yourself again. I'm just sorry I didn't realize sooner. I could have helped."

Stevie put a reassuring arm round his mum's shoulders. "It's OK, Mum. Seriously. I'm OK. And it's just gotta be done. It's as simple as that. We can't let the Shadowcasters win."

"All right, Stevie. I understand. You have powers beyond your age," she said, ruffling his hair as she used to do when he was younger, "and wisdom too."

"That's good, Sylvia," his aunt said, nodding. "Yes, yes…we've covered a lot of ground today and we will cover more in the days ahead. I am going to teach you all I know. And there is an Illuminator birth stone waiting for you. I've sent Bren Lee to get it…and a few other things we'll need before all this is through."

His mum looked out across the river, perhaps remembering her ordeal and the gentle voice that guided her away from danger. "You know it's unbelievable but in my heart I know it's true. I've always known it's true and it explains everything…Smithson…what's been happening here in Valley Dale. And something else?"

They both waited for her to speak.

"My premonitions. Dreams, I've had all my life…the ones I've been trying to bury and ignore. It makes sense now. It all makes sense. I've known all along what is going to happen, before it happens but I've buried that knowledge. Not any more though. But, Aunt Bessie, how on earth are we going to get into the Barron estate?"

They looked at each other, as if reading each other's mind.

"I think we know the answer to that, Sylvia," Aunt Bessie said. "You are going to tell us, aren't you?"

Sylvia thought for a moment. "Can I sleep on it?"

And then with the tension of the afternoon gone, they all laughed heartily as the afternoon sun disappeared over the horizon far out to sea.

Chapter 16

A Plan is Planned

The Vegas household slept soundly that night – every one of them. Sylvia had taken her husband aside when she returned home, and told him everything she knew about the danger the family was in, about the Illuminators and the Shadowcasters. Alexander Vegas took it all in with the calmness that was so characteristic of his steady nature. He tried to reason the story away but, like his wife, he knew in his heart it was true. He knew he had been living with a puzzle since the Barrons had entered their life. Now, he knew what that puzzle was and, more importantly, he knew how they were going to solve it.

But something worried him, the most practical, down to earth member of the Vegas family. If they had successfully stolen a cursed stone from the Barrons before, wouldn't the Shadowcasters expect them to do exactly the same thing again?

"How on earth do you think you will get past the Shadowcasters at the Barron estate," he said to Aunt Bessie that night over dinner of roast lamb and mint potatoes.

"Enjoying your lamb?" Aunt Bessie said and then, more quietly, "Remember Jem is in the kitchen helping to prepare dessert. He mustn't know our plans. I don't want to put him in a position of danger, where he would be forced to betray his own family."

"Ahh…yes…of course…" he mumbled, mopping up the last of the gravy with a piece of bread. He lowered his voice. "But how…how are you going to *get in*?"

Aunt Bessie smiled, mischief lighting up her eyes. "By doing the very thing they expect us not to do. They wouldn't think we'd be silly enough to try the same stunt twice…break into the Barron estate like we did in Smithson and steal the second cursed stone.

They will have it heavily guarded in any case, and it would be nearly impossible to break through the security surrounding the estate. But you know what, Alexander?"

"What, Aunt Bessie?" he said in a whisper, his eyes wide with anticipation.

"We are going to do the impossible…pull off the same trick twice and, the second time, with the element of surprise."

His dad looked totally unconvinced. "And the plan?" he said.

Aunt Bessie began clearing the dishes for dessert. "Well, now, that's up to Sylvia…"

"Sorry…what do you mean?" he said, helping her clear the plates too, and motioning to Stevie to turn the TV that he'd just turned on, off.

"Sylvia and her premonitions. I want her to dream a plan tonight, based on her visions of the future," Aunt Bessie said.

"So we follow the future plan, before it's been carried out."

"Precisely, Alexander, or we adapt it if we need to…so now we all need to get is a good night's sleep."

All his dad could do was shake his head and follow Aunt Bessie into the kitchen with an armful of dishes to be cleaned.

After dinner, the Vegas family went about their business quietly in the different parts of the house. Jem went to his room; Stevie offered to help his mum in the clinic with the nighttime medications for the animals in the vet hospital, and Alexander and Aunt Bessie did the dishes.

Around 10 pm Stevie and Jem were ushered off to bed, even though it was the beginning of school holidays. Aunt Bessie made Sylvia some chamomile tea to help her sleep. Only Alexander Vegas stayed up to watch the late night news.

"See you all in the morning," Sylvia said, carrying her steaming cup of tea up the stairs. "I'm feeling decidedly tired tonight. Busy day."

Aunt Bessie agreed. "It's time we turned in…yes, dear, I'm with you there."

That night, as darkness descended over the house, Aunt Bessie's sleeping potion slipped into her niece's cup of tea, ensured Sylvia went into a deep sleep, and dreamed…

Sylvia looked over at her husband as they were making their way up the long, winding driveway of the Barron estate. They drove slowly, taking in their surrounds. All around were the neatly manicured lawns and stone statues and monuments – grand and in keeping with the stately countenance of the house. In the back, Stevie and Mary Lou kept quite under the blanket, careful not to be seen.

Earlier that day Sylvia had phoned Chris Barron, insisting she and her husband meet him to try to put the past behind them. To her surprise Chris Barron had agreed.

As they drove, Sylvia felt the anxiety swirling in the pit of her stomach increase in intensity. What on earth were they all doing – Stevie and Mary Lou in the back of the car, and Aunt Bessie and Bren Lee waiting for Stevie to project his thoughts that the security had been turned off. She sent these thoughts firmly to the back of her mind and tried to concentrate on the charade they were all enacting. As the car came to the front door, Sylvia took a deep breath and looked over at her husband for support. Chris Barron was standing in the portico, waiting for them. As they got out of their car, Sylvia felt the darkness that was Chris Barron hit her like a punch in the stomach. She stumbled slightly, and Chris Barron was quick to take her arm.

"Allow me," he said, escorting Sylvia inside the house and motioning for Alexander to follow. Sylvia glanced back nervously at the car, hoping Stevie and Mary Lou would not be noticed.

Once inside, Sylvia looked desperately for her husband, but he was still talking to the man who was parking their car. She had no choice but to walk on with Chris Barron, loathing the feel of his cold, steely hand on her arm. His darkness was everywhere in the house. How had she not noticed it before in him? Heavy

drapes and subdued lighting gave the house an eerie atmos-
phere.

When they reached the library she noticed her husband was
not with her. Again she fought back the panic that threatened to
engulf her. They sat down by the fire, its flames surprisingly hot.
She drew her chair back a little.

"So, Sylvia," Chris Barron drawled. "What made you decide
to come and visit me, after everything that has gone before...in
Smithson? You were the last person I expected to call me. It must
be something very important to bring you here. Into my house."

She looked around for Alexander. What could be keeping
him?

"I...ahh...wanted to smooth things over...with you now
living in Valley Dale...coincidence isn't it?" she said.

Chris Barron drew his chair a little closer to hers, licking his
thin lips before he spoke and looking her so directly in the eyes,
that she thought she would be drawn into their blackness.

"It's no coincidence that I am here, my dear Sylvia. You know
that don't you? Did I tell you how lovely you are looking
tonight?"

She sat back in her chair, as far away from him as she could.
"Where is my husband?"

Chris Barron's dark eyes narrowed. He was confident
and...menacing. Sylvia suddenly felt very afraid.

"Oh, the ever faithful Alexander Vegas will be joining us
shortly, along with your son Stevie and his girl
pal...Mary...Mary Lou isn't it?"

She jumped – almost out of her chair, frightened and angry at
the same time.

"You..." she began.

But his sinister smile only widened. He was enjoying the
moment, she thought.

"Really, Sylvia, I thought you were more intelligent than to
attempt a half concocted plan to break into my house a second

time. Do you honestly think a man of my power would not find out about your childish plan," he said.

"But how?" she asked. "How did you know?"

His reply was quick. "Oh, I think you know that you have quite a talented, up and coming young Shadowcaster in your family. Young Jem is proving quite valuable to us…"

It was at that moment the room blackened and began to swirl and spin. The last thing she remembered was hearing someone screaming before the realization came that the screams were her own.

"Sylvia, Sylvia! Wake up! You're dreaming. Sylvia…it's OK, darling. Wake up. You're safe. You're at home."

Sylvia sat up focusing on her husband's voice, knowing she had been dreaming and trying to orientate herself with the comfort of her bedroom. Her husband put a gentle arm around her shoulders.

"Alexander. We simply can't break into the Barron estate. My dream…I saw it…we will be discovered…"

"But how?" Alexander said.

"We will be betrayed and caught by Chris Barron."

"But how," her husband persisted. "How would he know?"

Sylvia turned over, trying to hide the tears that were beginning to sting her eyes.

"Our son, Alexander. We will be betrayed by Jem."

Chapter 17

A Step in the Right Direction

The next morning the sun shone brightly through the kitchen windows, lightening an otherwise gloomy breakfast. Stevie helped himself to a large bowl of muesli with a liberal spoonful of the stewed peaches Aunt Bessie had made the day before. Jem was quiet, and a little sullen, while his mum and dad sat in silence drinking coffee. Aunt Bessie waited on the family smiling at them brightly, especially at his mum.

His dad was just about to leave to do a few home visits, and since school was on a midterm break, Jem would accompany him. After the two had left the kitchen, his mum let out a huge sigh of relief. "I didn't think they would ever go." And then more urgently: "Aunt Bessie, my dream."

Stevie finished his breakfast cereal and went and sat close by his mum. "It's OK, Mum. Isn't it, Aunt Bessie? It was just a dream."

Aunt Bessie pulled up a kitchen chair and handed her niece a cup of steaming tea. "There, Sylvie, drink the hot tea. It will make you feel better. I know about your dream last night." She looked over at Stevie.

"And you, Stevie, did you pick up on your mother's dream?"

Stevie nodded. Yes, it was as if I was there. We went to the Barron estate and we were caught. We simply can't allow that to happen to us in the future, Aunt Bessie," he said.

"Yes, Aunt Bessie, it is way too dangerous. Chris Barron knew of our plan to break into the estate because Jem told him. It is unthinkable that my son would ever betray his family," his mum said, urgency in her tone. She paused, looking to her aunt for reassurance, but Aunt Bessie sat quietly beside them.

His mum continued, as though she had unleashed a torrent of emotion, long held back by the events of the last year.

"I don't know what we can do," she said, beginning to cry. "I tried, I really tried to help, but the Barrons are one step in front of us. He has complete control at every turn. Even now as we sit here, having breakfast in our own house, he knows. He knows what we are planning because he has turned my son against us. Aunt Bessie what are we to do. Please tell us. How can we get the final cursed stone and rid ourselves of this nightmare?"

Aunt Bessie put a finger to her lips. "Shsh…Sylvia. You are allowing yourself to be consumed by fear. Stop for one moment and listen to your thoughts. What are you really hearing? Hmm? It's not that Chris Barron and the Shadowcasters will triumph and take everything they can from you…your two sons…your home…no listen closely and you will hear the determination of strength. The strength of an Illuminator. And an Illuminator bows to nobody. Fear darkens the mind when we submit obediently to what we know is wrong. And when we're fearful, the darkness spreads and dominates and our light, the light that allows us to follow our path, dims and, very soon, is extinguished. But we are not going to doubt ourselves, are we, Sylvia? I want you to know that, Sylvia, no matter what happens in the coming days, the light of the Illuminator will burn brightly. What you dreamed is one possible future, but not the absolute truth. Our futures are changing with the decisions we make in any one day, and with the choices we make. You have a rare and wonderful gift that is only just awakening in you. You can see the future and that gift is what will make the difference today to this family. Do you understand me, Sylvia, that what you dreamed is only one possible future?"

Sylvia nodded, focused intently on her aunt. Her eyes were bright with emotion, but she was no longer crying. She nodded, as if to say, 'I understand.' Stevie interrupted then.

"The way I see it, Mum, we change our plans and the future won't unfold the way you dreamed it would. That's right, isn't it, Aunt Bessie."

Aunt Bessie smiled at him. "Yes, dear, it's as simple as that. We will change our plans, based upon Sylvia's dream and create another possibility that's infinitely better than the one that is currently before us. In this possibility, we will be successful. I think that for our plan to work we will need the element of surprise. My sources at the Barron estate tell me that Chris Barron is planning a rather large party for the business community of Valley Dale at his estate. Now, we know that Mary Lou's father is a Shadowcaster, and the Hoods and also that new science teacher at your school, Stevie."

"Mr. Liechen! No...not him? He's half decent," Stevie said, surprise written across his face.

"Ah, so you think that Shadowcasters are all going to be spewing forth black shards from their auras and project dangerous, harmful thoughts and be in constant contact with the devil? No Stevie, Shadowcasters come in all shapes and sizes, but underneath their exteriors they are the same. They have a black mark on their soul, in this lifetime at least, and you won't have to dig too deeply to uncover the type of life they lead, as you will find negativity surrounds them, in their relationships and in the failed situations they have created for other people. Mr. Liechen is indeed a Shadowcaster and has been placed in Valley Dale school to protect Devlin Hood. And to keep a watchful eye on you, Stevie. But back to our plan Stevie...Sylvia?"

Sylvia poured another cup of tea. "I think best with a cup of tea in my hand," she said almost apologetically. "Well, if Chris Barron would know about me pretending to try and put the past behind us with a visit to his estate, I think we will need to try and get an invite to that party...somehow."

Stevie was thoughtful. "Well perhaps not an invite so much, as a way of getting into the estate because of the party."

"What do you mean?" his mum asked.

"Well, it's easy, Mum. If we could just get in with the caterers, for example, while the party is in full swing, we should be able to sneak into the eastern or western wings of the house and search for the cursed stone. What do you think of that, Aunt Bessie?"

Aunt Bessie nodded thoughtfully. "Yes, this could work. I do know that Bren Lee's mother has a catering business. If we could become waiters and waitresses for the night…that might work."

"Perhaps," his mum said. "But it's risky. Won't we be discovered? I mean Chris Barron knows who we are."

"Yes, but Chris Barron is not interested in meeting the domestic help. No, we will simply gain entrance to his estate long enough to locate the cursed stone…and my sources tell me it is deep within an ante-chamber in the west wing of the house, right near Jacob Barron's room."

At the mention of Jacob Barron's name, Stevie's blood turned cold. He shuddered at the thought of being so near to him. "But surely, Aunt Bessie, they will be guarding the stone? We simply cannot walk in and just take it."

"We are not going to take risks, Stevie. I have someone working for us, located in that house. She is a friend and I trust her. She has told me that the cursed stone is not guarded because it doesn't have to be. As it is Jacob's stone, the stone that is connected to his soul, Jacob's close proximity is enough. The stone and its master are connected and one will always know where the other is," Aunt Bessie said.

"Then how are we going to take it," his mum said.

"Yeah, Aunt Bessie? Seems like we are attempting the impossible," Stevie interjected.

"Perhaps, if we were to separate them. But we're not. We will take Jacob with us."

Stevie's jaw dropped. "Take him with us. You can't be serious."

Aunt Bessie nodded. "I am very serious Stevie. Stone and master will leave the mansion that night and by morning we will have destroyed the stone. When its power has been destroyed, then Jacob Barron's power too will be diminished. If our plan works, Stevie, you won't have to watch out for Jacob Barron ever again. And I have a little extra something up our sleeves that I cannot reveal to you both…well at least not yet. But I will say, Bren Lee's recent trip away for me has been successful. While we will be relying on our powers, we will also have the power of something else; an ancient amulet of the Illuminators that belongs to Sylvia. So you see, we are not going into the Barron estate completely empty handed."

As the morning wore on, the group of three planned the details of the raid carefully. Stevie's dad would remain behind with Jem. Aunt Bessie would be part of the waiting staff and Stevie and Mary Lou would get roles as kitchen hands. Bren Lee would pull some strings with his family to get them in, and help them search for the stone when the time came. Aunt Bessie's source at the Barron estate would let them into the west wing of the house.

His mum sat thoughtfully. "Well that's everyone accounted for. What about me? What part do I play?"

Aunt Bessie grinned cheekily. "Well, this is where it gets interesting. You are going to that party, Sylvia – I will see you are invited, and you are going to keep Chris Barron busy while we take the cursed stone."

"Oh, my goodness," his mum said, shocked at the suggestions. "Umm…I'm not sure I can pull that off."

Aunt Bessie patted her hand reassuringly. "Of course you can, dear. You have to go, because just as Stevie and I 'read' your dream last night, so too did Jem, and he will communicate this to the Barrons tonight when he sees Devlin Hood."

"But…isn't that what we want to avoid?" his mum said.

"No, it isn't. You see Chris Barron will think you are coming to the party to take the stone, under the same circumstances as your dream of the future. Meanwhile, we have changed the plans. He does not know that Mary Lou, Bren Lee, Stevie and I, will also be there. You see, Sylvia, in dreaming of the future last night, we are able to change it today. Nothing is ever pre-determined. We always have choice, and choices change the future."

Stevie shifted in his seat. It was starting to make sense now – he was beginning to see how they could pull it off. "It just might work," he said. "How many weeks do we have before the party?" he said, looking directly at his aunt. "We need to be sure it's going to work."

His aunt, always one to look on the bright side, let out a hearty laugh. "Weeks, my boy? We have a matter of days only. Days to get Mary Lou ready for her part, and Bren Lee to play his part. And for us to undertake our training."

"Training?" his mum asked, entirely exhausted with the morning's excitement.

"Yes, my dear, we must train to strengthen our thoughts and remove all fear. As three, we must be strong." Aunt Bessie said.

"The unbreakable circle," Stevie whispered more to himself.

"How do you know about that," his aunt asked.

"I don't know...I really don't know. It just came into my mind," he said.

"Umm. That's strange, Stevie, I've told you about the power of three but not about the unbreakable circle. You are, or were, not ready for that. But now...well let's just say circumstances have changed."

"...When the circle is unbroken...when you are all one with each other, protect each other as three, then you are strong as one."

"Precisely, Stevie," Aunt Bessie said. "Of all the dynamics that can occur in groups, three is the most dangerous, and yet, when three can become as one, it is also the most powerful."

"Then we are three," his mum said, sipping her tea slowly, deep in thought.

Aunt Bessie smiled confidently. "And of course, Sylvia, you will have your amulet."

Chapter 18

The Unbreakable Circle

Stevie shot the stone at Mary Lou's window with as much accuracy as he could muster. It went k-thump and then ricocheted onto the lattice, before hitting the ground below. He hoped that the stone would not disturb Mary Lou's father whom he knew was reading the Valley Dale news in the lounge room below.

He was on his way home from the skatepark when, on impulse, he turned down into Elm Street. It hadn't changed in all the months he'd been visiting Mary Lou – dark, shadowed and definitely creepy. Stevie tried to keep his mind on the simple skate practice he was allowed to do now with his wrist mending well, but it was impossible. His grinds and his flips were slow and lacked precision. He just couldn't stop thinking about the coming weekend and Chris Barron's party, and the ruse they were planning to pull off. At the heart of his concern was not just the imminent danger they were all in, but also the thought of meeting his nemesis Jacob Barron again. It had been a year since they had battled at Smithson's Skateopia and Stevie well remembered that last second he looked into Jacob's eyes, before his trick went horribly wrong. He remembered the absolute hatred and malice that Jacob had for him and he knew too, that in that defining moment before Jacob fell, his life changed forever.

It had been a long road from Smithson to the present moment. As he stood looking up at Mary Lou's window – waiting for her to appear and wave down to him as usual – he thought silently about how different it was for his family now. But he didn't blame himself anymore, nor curse the fact he was an Illuminator. Rather, he accepted who he was and who he knew he would become…one day. That was, of course, if he survived what was coming. Stevie had always known he would have to face Jacob Barron again – knew it the first time he heard the whispering voices on the wind, coming to him from behind the veil. A shroud of darkness that was Jacob's unconscious. He shuddered in the fading night, wishing Mary Lou would hurry. He threw another stone and this time there was a faint movement from behind the window before Mary Lou flung it open, a huge grin on her face. Stevie stopped for barely a second, as he caught the thought that she was glad to see him and he couldn't help but respond. Of all the bad things that had happened this year, meeting Mary Lou was not one of them.

"Hey, you," she said softly, trying not to draw attention to themselves.

"Yeah, hey, you," he whispered back. "Wanna go for a skate?"

She laughed. "What, me? Skate? You're kiddin' aren't you? I'm not sure I could stay on that board. But I'll tell you what – I've got my old rollerblades in the cupboard. Hang on a tick."

She was back soon enough, holding the blades up like a trophy, and then throwing them out to land on the ground beside Stevie. Opening the window wide enough to allow her through, she shimmied down the lattice beside her window and jumped the last two yards, landing on her feet.

Stevie picked up the skates and dropped his skateboard, catching it with his foot. "Here, you can put these on round the corner." And with that he grabbed her hand and they ran into the growing darkness. They had about an hour before dinner, and he didn't want to waste any time.

"Hey, Vegas. What are you doin'? It's nearly tea time and you just turn up to my house. What am I s'pposed to think?" Mary Lou said a touch of humor in her tone.

Stevie couldn't help notice the smile on Mary Lou's face. She seemed happy to see him despite his random visit to her house.

"Sorry. I…err…didn't mean to shock you. I was just passing, you know after skate practice and I saw your light on. Thought

I'd take a walk down friendly Elm Street…"

She giggled. "Shsh, Stevie, someone might hear you; well hear your thoughts. Let's get out of here quick. I don't want my father knowing you're here."

He stopped once they got round the corner for her to put on her skates. She sat down quickly on the grassy footpath.

"No really. I mean what brings you here," she said, the smile gone from her face. "Is something wrong?"

He smiled at her, noticing for the first time the particular way her long blonde hair fell past her shoulders. It was pretty hair, shiny and soft even in the unnatural light of the street lamp. She was wearing a pink shirt with her jeans tonight. An odd color for her, he thought, given pink was a feminine color and Mary Lou tried very hard not to be thought of as a girl. She was more the tough tomboy who could ride, and run, like a boy.

She got up gingerly at first on her blades. "I told you. I haven't worn these things in an eon. Let's take it slow for a while."

"Sure," he said, gently propelling the skateboard with one foot along the sidewalk, keeping pace with her as she rollerbladed. "I…just need to talk for a while," he said, looking at her from underneath his long fringe. He pushed his fringe to the side and stood straight on his board. No matter how many times he skated, he still loved it with a passion.

Mary Lou rollerbladed alongside him, waiting patiently for him to talk. The more she skated the better she got at it. "So, Stevie, I know you pretty well by now – what's on your mind?"

Stevie glanced sideways, all the while trying to keep a close eye on her blading. The last thing he wanted was for her to fall and hurt herself.

"Oh, you know, just minor stuff like breaking into the Barron estate. Should be a real breeze," he said.

"Oh, that," she said. "You know I used to worry all the time about the Shadowcasters – that was until my mum died. They came for her, and in the end there was nothing we could do…or so I thought. You know what, Stevie?"

He gave her his full concentration. "What?"

"I discovered there was plenty I could do. Spy on them for Aunt Bessie for one. Be vigilant and never let them get away with anything if I could help it. I used to be frightened of them, but the truth is that unless you have people standing up to them, then they are free to use their power against Illuminators, and against everyone. And I don't want people to suffer like I did."

She stopped skating, and he did too. They had come, unknowingly to a street near where Bren Lee lived.

"You thinking what I'm thinking?" Stevie said.

"Yep," she replied. "Let's go and pay Bren Lee a visit and talk over the plans for this weekend. You might feel better if we do."

"OK. Bren Lee will probably have me meditate or something. He thinks everything can be solved by going a bit Zen."

She laughed and tugged at his arm. When they got to Bren's house behind the gym, Stevie again threw a stone at the bedroom window and, like a flash, Bren Lee appeared. "I'll be down in two secs," he whispered.

Before long, he appeared at his side door – no shimmying down the lattice for him, but rather a more dignified exit.

"What's up, you two?" he whispered into the night air, aware that it was getting late.

Stevie motioned him over to the nearby sidewalk. "Sorry, mate, don't mean to disturb you. I wanted to talk about the plans for this weekend. I know you and Aunt Bessie have been planning it, but I dunno. There's a lot at risk."

Bren Lee looked at them, a small smile playing at the corners of his mouth.

"Hey, don't worry. We've planned it well. Nothing will go wrong. You shouldn't worry Stevie…or you, Mary Lou. I'd be more worried if we were doing nothing, because even as we speak, the Shadowcasters are getting stronger. The word from my contacts is that they are planning something for next week's lunar eclipse – we don't know what, but they are gathering and meeting at the Barron estate on the night of the party."

Stevie sucked in his breath, aware of the need not to show any fear in front of Mary Lou. He didn't want her upset. As if reading his thoughts, she replied, "I agree Bren. There is more to worry about if we don't get the last cursed stone."

"Precisely," he said, and then looking at Stevie. "You know, Stevie, you are braver than you think."

"It's not me I'm worried about Bren. It's Jem. Day by day he grows closer to Devlin Hood. They are nearly inseparable now and his aura is mostly grey. I'm scared that he will turn permanently into a Greycaster, or worse, become a Shadowcaster. Already, I know he's been bullying kids at school with Devlin Hood and his gang. Jem is now in danger of being no better than them. And all this, when he was bullied himself. I just can't understand it – it's like he's someone I don't know."

Mary Lou looked away. If anybody knew about the rite of passage into the wrong side of right and wrong, it was her. With Shadowcasting blood running through her veins, she had fought the battle against her dark side...and won. She was now more Illuminator than perhaps anyone else. She placed a gentle hand on Stevie shoulder.

"I'm with Bren Lee. If we don't do anything, Jem's fate is sealed. I'm afraid, Stevie with his past, the many times he's been a victim himself, there is a danger he'll want to do to others what has been done to him."

"Instead of taking aim at the bullies themselves?" Stevie questioned.

She nodded, as did Bren Lee. "Yes, unfortunately. Everybody chooses their own path and not everybody gets it right the first time. Trouble is that the Shadowcasters are leading him down a path where there is no return."

Stevie's eyes blazed with anger. "No. Not while I'm around. I just don't accept that Jem is not one of us. There is still time to reach him. I won't abandon my brother. I'm telling you. I will fight for him, against anyone – Jacob Barron, Devlin Hood. I don't care how strong they are, or how many cursed stones they have…my brother will not become a Shadowcaster."

Bren Lee's eyes softened. "No one is asking you to abandon your brother, Stevie, but you do see how important it is that we act now?"

"And save Jem," Mary Lou said.

He nodded, understanding that so much was riding on the success of their plan to take away the Shadowcasters power source – the last cursed stone, and save not only Jem but anyone in the future who was vulnerable to a Shadowcaster's will.

"Then bring it on," Stevie said. "Let's end this once and for all."

Chapter 19

Shadows Fall

Night was beginning to fall on the Vegas household. A world away, the Barron estate was buzzing with activity as caterers began to ready Chris Barron's party for Valley Dale residents. One caterer, Bren Lee, paced the kitchen trying to stay calm. Would their plan work? He had been far more confident the other night with Stevie and Mary Lou than he felt now, in the Barrons' large, gleaming kitchen. He was lucky his mother's catering firm had been contracted for the job. Already, he had made contact with the Illuminators who had been sent to help them take the cursed stone. But despite their careful planning, Bren Lee had a feeling deep in the pit of his stomach, something wasn't right. He closed his eyes briefly and breathed deeply, sending waves of calm through his body. As a martial arts instructor he knew the importance of discipline in the face of danger.

Beginning to organize the endless trays of food that were being delivered to the back of the estate on large, gleaming platters, he quickly checked his watch. In 30 minutes he would meet Aunt Bessie, Stevie and Mary Lou at the west gate. He prayed that his contact would be able to turn off the security cameras, momentarily, at that time to avoid their detection. Everything about their plan hung on a multitude of actions that, at any time, could go wrong.

"Excuse me. Are you from the catering firm and in charge of this evening's menu?" His thoughts were interrupted by an authoritative voice from behind. He swiveled to see Chris Barron standing at the entrance to the kitchen. Although Bren Lee was no Illuminator, he was sensitive enough to be able to feel the darkness that emanated from his employer. Mentally, he put up a white light and closed his thoughts off. It was imperative Chris Barron, an expert mind reader, knew nothing of their plan.

"Yes…sir, you may speak to me," he said, bowing deferentially and giving Chris Barron his full attention.

He felt Chris Barron sizing him up, probing his mind, as was a Shadowcaster's custom with all strangers. Bren had made sure the Lee catering firm was very well recommended, but he could see the slight mistrust in Chris Barron's eyes. He knew the Barrons would be extra careful, particularly since Stevie and Aunt Bessie's theft of the cursed stone. He hoped his white light shield would not arouse suspicion in Chris Barron. Well he hoped…

"The first of the guests are arriving, please put out the salmon and crab canapés."

Bren Lee nodded, again with a slight bow. Chris Barron looked at him intently for a moment, trying again to read his thoughts, and without luck turned and walked away.

Bren Lee let out a sigh of relief and motioned to his mother who was now putting out the canapés that he needed to check the catering truck. Trying not to attract any attention to himself, he slipped out the back door. He was already five minutes late for his rendezvous with Stevie and Mary Lou.

He hoped his friends were faring better than he was, but he had no way of knowing whether or not they had run into trouble. Mary Lou and Stevie had taken their time getting ready that morning but were still on schedule, and Stevie's dad Alexander was to take Jem and his dog to the park to keep Jem safe and away from the Shadowcasters. He knew Stevie's mum Sylvia would getting ready for the evening at the Barron estate, and that meeting Chris Barron would be hard for her. Against every fiber of her being she had contacted Chris Barron that week to 'try to put the past behind them.' Chris Barron had responded welcomingly, by inviting her to attend his upcoming party.

Aunt Bessie had assured everyone, including Stevie's mum

that because they had changed Sylvia's dream enough, the outcome would be different. They would not get caught by Chris Barron. He would be expecting Mary Lou and Stevie to be in the back of the Vegas car – and he would expect Stevie's parents, not just his mum.

Aunt Bessie's plan was risky to say the least – planting a dream vision in Chris Barron's mind and hoping he would believe it, while the real plan unfolded meant that the slightest detail of their plan had to work. At any point, Chris Barron's suspicions would be raised.

Stevie and Mary Lou had walked slowly through the forest to the estate that morning – knowing that their plan hung on a knife's edge.

"Where is he?" Stevie muttered under his breath, loosening the collar of his catering staff uniform. He usually wore jeans and a T-shirt, but tonight he was dressed in checked pants and a collared shirt – the uniform of the Lee catering service.

"Just be patient," Mary Lou whispered. She too was in her catering uniform, which felt odd against her skin. Like Stevie, she was more comfortable in jeans and a biker's leather jacket. She focused on her surroundings. "Sshh, Stevie, now is not the time to panic."

Just when Stevie thought he would explode with anticipation, Bren Lee's face appeared at the side gate.

"Come on you two. The security cameras are only off for two minutes. We must make for the garden shed quickly."

With that they were away, running at full stride, aware the clock was ticking.

They made for the old building used to store gardening equipment with only seconds to spare. Stevie could sense the Shadowcasters' thoughts very near...near enough, surely, for Chris Barron to discover Stevie's thoughts. His hand went instinctively to his necklace as it always did when he was in danger – he imagined himself surrounded in white light and extended that to Mary Lou. She crouched calmly next to him, waiting for their next move. All her years of motorbike riding and her independent streak meant she was used to taking responsibility and that made her courageous, particularly in dangerous situations. Today, she was courageous. She felt the white light of Stevie's thoughts encircle her, providing the 'thought' protection she needed from the Shadowcasters who were currently inside the estate, including her father.

"OK," Bren Lee whispered. "We've got exactly two minutes to make it to the west wing side door. Even though we look like we are supposed to be here in our uniforms, the west wing is definitely off limits to us. If we are even a second out, the alarms will trigger. Do you understand me, Stevie? And you are on your own now. I've got to get back and meet Aunt Bessie. She'll be coming in any minute with the last catering van. Quickly, go. Go now."

Stevie shot Bren a quick smile and grabbing Mary Lou's hand, took off at full pace, crouching low past the drawing room's big French doors. Hugging the wall to stay out of view from the upstairs rooms, the west wing entrance finally came into sight. Mary Lou checked her watch – 10 seconds to spare. Stevie dived for the door, hoping to find it unlocked…and it was. Four, three, two seconds…they finally closed the door behind them and leaned panting up against it. Inside the library, all was dark and Stevie sensed an evil nearby he had never felt before. It was as if the devil himself had come out from the bowels of the earth. His Illuminator stone began to pulsate against his skin, as if getting ready to dispel the nearby darkness.

"Where's Aunt Bessie?" Mary Lou whispered. She too was beginning to feel her fear. It was growing in proportion with the pure evil she felt. She glanced at Stevie, and then at the far corner door where the darkness was at its thickest. She could just make it out and the beginnings of a small hallway, beyond which she knew was Jacob Barron's bedroom, and inside, the small antechamber that held the cursed stone.

"Aunt Bessie," Stevie called, sending his thoughts outward. She was now two minutes late, but there was no response. Stevie did not even sense her presence on the estate.

Aunt Bessie, meanwhile, was having troubles of her own. She had been on her way to the estate in the Lee catering van, sitting amongst the rumbling trays of caviar and dainty canapés of every description, when she felt a piercing pain her left temple, as though a very powerful mind probe was trying to gain entry to her thoughts. Immediately the thought of Devlin Hood's father, Blake, entered her mind. She steeled herself against the mind probe. How would Blake Hood have known her location? She sent out her own gentle probe, disguised behind the thoughts of another elderly woman attending the party, whom Aunt Bessie had identified at the far gate of the estate as Mrs. Rosemary Barden. The thoughts she projected were merely thoughts about who might be attending the party from Valley Dale's social elite. Immediately, Aunt Bessie located Blake Hood inside, alongside Mary Lou's father and Chris Barron. She sensed the shadowy presence of several other Shadowcasters, including Mr. Liechen, but also the trusted group of Illuminators she had planted inside the estate. And the quiet, but worried thoughts of Bren Lee who was, again, pacing Chris Barron's gleaming steel kitchen, waiting for her.

She motioned to the van driver to pull over. There had to be a change of plan if she was to succeed in getting into the estate without being seen. Blake Hood's attempted mind probe had unsettled her, as it was entirely unexpected. And more so, that she had felt it inside the catering van. Did Chris Barron suspect their plan? She searched the thoughtscape of the estate's guests and found no indication their plan had been discovered. The driver of the van had let her off at the side entrance to the estate.

She could see the west wing door through the grill of the gate, and she wondered how on earth she was going to get through. There was a vague possibility…she had never tried it before – levitation, only heard about it. At 63 years of age, there was not much Aunt Bessie couldn't do as a senior member of the Luminous, but levitation was something only one or two Illuminators had done in the history of their group. Once levitation was achieved, it was possible to apparate but that, again, had not been achieved by anyone but the original Luminous, thousands of years earlier.

Aunt Bessie saw no other answer than to try levitation. She knew the longer she delayed, the more perilous it became for Stevie, Mary Lou and now Sylvia, inside the Barron estate. She closed her eyes and let the moment still within her. As if time itself had stopped, she imagined herself weightlessly rising as she had done in the past, in her dreams. At first she felt herself rise only inches and every time she took her concentration, and confidence, off gaining momentum she came crashing to the ground. She tried one last time. Stilling her mind, she felt the thrill of the levitation beginning to work. Higher, higher, only two more inches to clear the estate wall. As soon as that thought entered her head, she began to fall but was quick enough to reach out to the ledge. Pulling herself up to lie on the wall's ledge was a feat in itself. She wasn't as fit as she had been even 10 years ago. Perched flat on top of the wall to avoid being seen, she wondered how on earth she was going to get from the top of the wall to the ground below. As if reading her thoughts, Bren Lee appeared out of the shadows. She had never been so pleased to see anyone before, and particularly the extension ladder he had perched on his shoulders. She wouldn't be trying to apparate tonight; levitation was enough.

"How did you know I was here?" she whispered down to him.

He shook his head. "You are not the only one who can read minds, Aunt Bessie," he whispered. "I might not be an

Illuminator, but a trained warrior nonetheless and I know when both enemy and friend are coming."

Once safely down, she smiled at him. "Thank you," she said, simply.

"That's OK. My pleasure," he whispered. "But, Aunt Bessie, we must hurry. This was not in the plan and we risk being caught."

"No," she said, hurrying to keep up with him. "It wasn't in the plan, but I suspect that this night will not go according to plan and we must be on our guard, and ready at a moment's notice to adapt to changing circumstances. Did you bring what I asked?"

"Yes," Bren Lee said. "I have the amulet hidden. It's here when we need it."

Aunt Bessie nodded. "Good…good work. We may yet need it before the night is through."

As they reached the west wing door, Aunt Bessie sent a thought projection to Stevie inside.

"Thank God," Stevie whispered to Mary Lou. "Aunt Bessie and Bren Lee are nearly here."

Mary Lou pointed at the corner door and to the blackness which was encircling it. "Not before time," she whispered. "Look, Stevie. Look!"

Stevie looked over in the direction she was pointing and couldn't believe what he saw. The blackness was growing and appeared alive with pulsating shards projecting outward in an ever expanding circle.

At that instant, Stevie's thoughts were drawn to his mother.

Chapter 20

A Dangerous Moon Before the Dawn

Sylvia arrived at the Barron estate on schedule. She steeled herself while driving, focusing only on the coming evening. If she played her part correctly, her sons would be safe by morning. That was all she cared about now. The long year since Smithson had been difficult. Learning her sons were in danger had been agonizing and she could do little to protect them against the unknown powers of the Shadowcasters. She had been out of her depth, until now. Now she knew she was an Illuminator. She felt the light within her and acknowledged it; accepted it. She was eager to put her powers to use in protecting her sons. Her heart sank every time she thought of Jem…her baby, under the influence of the Shadowcasters. How could her life…her family, once so normal be in mortal danger now? But asking why was pointless. It was her actions now that could help her sons. She knew that. And so she steeled herself against her loathing for Chris Barron, as she drove through the estate's gates. Following the winding road towards the front portico, she refused to be overawed by the sheer size and grandeur of the estate. Of course, Chris Barron would have the biggest house in town – money and power need to be on show and visible for all to see, she thought wryly.

She steeled herself as she pulled up in front of the waiting valet, and surrounded herself with a protective white aura, a technique Aunt Bessie had taught her days earlier. Already she had mastered many things. She had committed herself to the training with Stevie and Aunt Bessie in the last few days. They were strengthening the power of three, which Aunt Bessie had said, was an ancient ritual of the Illuminators. By focusing their will onto one thought, they could summon the power of the storm – wind, rain and the electrical power of lightning could be manifested…if they were strong enough. At first when they tried, small spots of rain had appeared, but as they practiced, hour after hour, the wind had risen. On their final training session there had been a short burst of lightning. But there was no more time with the party looming. Sylvia hoped their practice had been enough.

"Good evening, Sylvia." A deep voice from behind interrupted her thoughts. She remembered to mentally strengthen her white cloak of protection. She did not want Chris Barron probing her mind and picking up thoughts about their plan – the last thing she wanted was to betray her family. She straightened, aware the black silk dress she had chosen for the party was very glamorous against her blonde hair. She tightened the burgundy, fine wool shawl around her shoulders, as Chris Barron's gaze fell on the whiteness of her skin. She smiled with a confidence she didn't feel.

"You look stunning tonight, Sylvia. But where is Alexander?" he said, taking her arm and guiding her inside.

She steeled herself against his touch. "Ah, Alex is at home with Jem. I'm afraid you have only me tonight as your guest."

His arm went to her waist. "A prospect I'm indeed enchanted by."

Again she smiled, aware of the false charm that hid her real feelings…the part of her that wanted to harm this man for the havoc he had wreaked on her family. She pushed the thoughts to the back of her mind. "You are too gracious a host, Chris. Umm, I'm aware we parted on…strained circumstances in Smithson but I was hoping that by attending tonight, we might find a way to put the past behind us. Don't you agree?"

He looked at her rather sharply for an instant, but the mask of gracious host soon returned. They had reached the estate's ballroom where hundreds of guests were enjoying the Barrons' hospitality.

"I completely agree, Sylvia," he said, motioning for a waiter to bring them drinks. "Now, if I may, I would like to introduce you to some of my friends. After all, you are a very special guest tonight."

Within moments, Blake Hood appeared, along with Mr. Liechen, Stevie's English teacher at school.

"Sylvia Vegas, these are two of my dear friends. Blake Hood, whom I understand is your neighbor and Mr. Liechen our local teacher extraordinaire."

She took a deep sip of the champagne that had just been given to her. "Umm, yes how are you, Blake? Settling into Valley Dale life?"

Blake Hood was dressed in black, as usual. Sylvia had rarely seen him in any other color. His receding blond hair did nothing to hide a prominent forehead and hawkish dark eyes. Sylvia had disliked him the instant she had met him when he had knocked on her back door, asking for the name of a good plumber. She hadn't let him in that day, and was quite rude to him, based only on a feeling of unease in his company. Tonight was no different.

"Yes," he replied. "Valley Dale has been very good to me and particularly given my very good friend Chris Barron has now moved here."

Mr. Liechen stepped a little closer to the group. "Yes, Mrs. Vegas, Valley Dale has had a bit of a population surge in recent months with new arrivals. Tell me, how is our resident skate-boarding star going?"

"And your other son, Jem?" Blake Hood asked. "He really is a very intelligent little boy."

Sylvia could hardly stop herself from heading to the front door again and leaving the party. She sensed the malevolence in her company, and wished herself anywhere but at the Barron party. But she had a job to do, and that was keep Chris Barron occupied for as long as she could tonight.

"Thank you, Blake…and Mr. Liechen. Both my sons are doing

extremely well. Now, if you'll excuse me I would like a quick word with our host."

Chris Barron, faintly surprised by Sylvia's request for a private conversation with him, nodded. "Yes, of course, we can go to the library if you'd like."

The three men exchanged quick glances that Sylvia caught, as she followed Barron towards the library. Closing the door behind them Barron motioned to the high backed, leather chairs in front of the fire. Sylvia felt a familiarity with this scene, like déjà vu, and she remembered she had 'seen' it in her dream. A moment of panic gripped her, but she shook off the feeling of panic – nothing was predetermined, she remembered. The future changes with our choices and they had deviated from her dream…Barron's voice cut through her thoughts and she remembered where she was.

"A beautiful moon tonight, Sylvia," he said, pouring her a generous brandy. She accepted it graciously, determined to keep up the pretense as long as was needed.

"Yes, Chris – a full moon actually…"

"Beautiful. It reminds me of my childhood actually," he said. "We would gather late at night under its night light – play I mean, as children. Ah, yes, the light of a moon is nearest to the day when one can see a shadow even in the dark."

Sylvia sat back in the high chair and let the soft light of the fire warm her. She was cold with apprehension and its warmth somehow comforted her. So much rested on tonight's outcome.

"I suppose you want to know what I wanted to talk to you about tonight, Chris."

"I had wondered, Sylvia…and while I didn't want to be rude I do have guests…but I jump ahead, what is it you wanted to see me about?"

Sylvia sipped her drink slowly, trying to buy time. For every moment she kept Chris Barron occupied, was one less moment Stevie, Mary Lou and Aunt Bessie risked discovery.

She cleared her throat, stalling for time. "I just wanted to say that I hope that there are no hard feelings from last summer…I mean it was a skateboarding accident and it could quite as easily been Stevie as Jacob. I'm so sorry your son was injured. How is he now? I had heard you brought him here to Valley Dale, but that he was still in a coma."

He stood with his back to her, and she couldn't read his face. "Thank you for your concern, Sylvia. Please know there are no ill feelings toward you…no, not at all towards you."

She stood up, placing her hand on his shoulder. "I'm truly sorry about Jacob. I just want us all to go on with our lives." And, somewhere within herself, she actually meant that.

He turned and faced her then, the softness that had been in his tone a minute earlier, draining away just as quickly as water rushes down a sink.

"I do not think that we can do that, Sylvia. You see your son Stevie is responsible for my son's illness. Even now he would not lie in a coma if it was not for…"

He straightened and only the sound of the fire crackling in the grate broke the silence.

She moved towards the door, aware now there was no fooling Chris Barron, and what was obvious was he would never forgive or forget the skateboarding accident, blaming Stevie for what had happened. "I'm sorry; it was a mistake to speak of Jacob's accident. I was only trying to tell you that my son Stevie was not to blame, and somehow hope that you bared no grudge."

He turned around then, his face angry and menacing. His eyes were ablaze and Sylvia could see the dark outline of his aura. But more so, she could feel the venom buried deep within him. She knew now that there would be no forgiveness, or leniency, for her son.

She moved closer to the door, ready to leave, aware that Chris Barron was dangerous in this mood. "Again I'm sorry. I'll be just getting back to the party now. Please don't trouble yourself any further.

He moved towards her, the menace in his face stronger, darker and more threatening.

"Leave, Sylvia Vegas? I don't think so. You will be going nowhere tonight. Tonight you are my…guest."

She felt nothing more as the room darkened and she slipped out of consciousness. Her last thought was for the moon, its rays permeating the heavy curtains as if trying unsuccessfully to drive back the shadows. A far off voice seemed to caution her. 'But we all know that the moon's light is just an illusion.'

Chapter 21

Behind the Veil

Stevie and Mary Lou hugged the wall, watching the shadows surrounding the door to Jacob Barron's room grow and expand towards them. The shadows held such darkness and black, swirling energy that they were both driven back, wondering how they would get beyond it. Mary Lou shivered and gripped her stomach. Whatever was in there was making her feel sick, and faint. The black shadows were disorienting her and she stumbled against the wall.

"Mary Lou," Stevie whispered urgently. "Are you all right? You're as white as a sheet."

She put her head back and closed her eyes, sucking in the air as though it was her last breathe. The shadows inched their way slowly towards them.

"No, I'm not all right, Stevie. It's like the darkness is swallowing me up. I…don't feel myself. I can hear voices, whispering like they are from hell itself. Ah…I don't under-stand…why they are affecting me so. The whispering is getting louder. Stevie…"

She slumped against the wall, and slid down to the floor, barely conscious.

Stevie crouched down beside his friend and smoothed back her long hair, which had fallen over her face. He didn't like to see his friend in trouble. Concentrating on the blackness he projected his thoughts outward, like a white shield between It and him. Mary Lou took another breath and some of the color returned to her face.

"That's better, Stevie…I feel as if I can breathe now. It was as if I was choking on that thing. What on earth is it?"

"I don't know, Mary Lou, but I could hear the whispering too.

I've been hearing it, off and on, since Jacob Barron's accident at the skatepark over 12 months ago. I think…I'm not entirely sure, but I think he's made a deal with the devil," Stevie said.

Mary Lou coughed, still struggling with the blackness despite Stevie's shield.

"I don't know, Stevie, but I can hear the whispering inside my head too. It feels like that blackness is sucking me into its depths. Maybe it's my Shadowcasting and Illuminator blood, but I don't think I can go any further, Stevie. I'm sorry."

Stevie put an arm around her shoulder. "It's OK, Mary Lou. I've always known that I would have to face Jacob Barron alone. It is my…responsibility, I suppose. It's what I have to do."

Mary Lou shook her head. "No, Stevie, you can't. You mustn't. We'll wait until Aunt Bessie and Bren Lee come."

Stevie went to get up. "No, Mary Lou. This is between Jacob and me. I don't want to put anyone else in danger any more. It's about me. It's always been about me."

She grabbed his arm. "You don't know what's in there, Stevie."

He shook her off. "Oh, I have a pretty good idea. It's Jacob Barron and his cursed stone and a whole lot of dark power coming from another place. I've known about this for months now. Known that I have to face this myself. Alone."

And with that he was off, disappearing through the darkness, leaving Mary Lou behind to watch as the black, pulsating mass swallowed him up. He sensed her fading thoughts acknowledging his bravery and felt a burst of her white protective energy directed at him which did little to shield him from the looming abyss.

As Stevie dived into the blackness, he was struck by the massive temperature drop within the mass but he could still hear the voices, louder this time and unmistakably the voice of Jacob Barron and something else – a Shadowcaster of immense power. He pushed forward, feeling no fear. It was as if he was on the biggest skateboard ramp of his life. He knew he had to keep going. He couldn't see in front, but was drawn to his left. Feeling for the door, he pushed it open. In the middle of the room lay Jacob Barron, as if in a coma, and to his left a black stone pulsating with a very powerful energy. But beyond Jacob and the cursed stone was a passageway, its entrance carved in the rock; and at the end of the long, dark passage, a deep blue, almost black energy field. That was where the whispering was coming from.

He hugged the side wall and inched past the cursed stone, wishing Aunt Bessie was with him. Although his necklace was glowing with a hot, white protective light and he was projecting his own white shield, which pulsated with the power of the universe, he felt the blackness surround him deep within his soul, and all the while the whispering growing louder.

"He comes, master. At last, he comes…your will is my will. I will do what needs to be done…"

Stevie felt the fear in the pit of his stomach, and fought against it. He would not give into fear, not let it run away with him. He steadied himself in the moment and concentrated on the passageway, and trying to get to it. He reached the passageway within seconds and began to walk toward the bluey-black light, despite his fear. Stevie Vegas was no coward and whether it was a 10 yard skateboard jump, or an unknown passageway with evil at its end, he didn't care. He had only one thought in his head and that was to finish it once and for all…and he was prepared to pay the price. He only knew he was done with looking over his shoulder for Shadowcasters; done with seeing his family and friends suffer, and done with living a half-life. He wanted his old life back, and if facing the evil would end it once and for all, then he would tackle it head on and take the consequences.

As he moved through the passageway, he glimpsed a dark, hooded shape in what looked like an antechamber. The dark shape raised its hooded head and Stevie saw nothing but blackness and the yellow like eyes of a tiger. Wild, merciless eyes, Stevie thought, that looked straight into his eyes without fear or emotion. They were the eyes of a killer.

"So you come, Stevie Vegas," It hissed. "I have waited a long time for this moment – since you were born. You are the one, born into light that turns willingly toward the dark. It is you who forsakes all hope, all grace, all love and all light. Are you surprised to hear what I know?"

Stevie was less than three yards from the Shadowcaster, but he was brave, braver than the entity gave him credit for. He reached deep within toward the light that was burning in a far off place, somewhere inside him. The long months of worry about his family…about Jem and the constant presence of the Shadowcasters had worn him down, but he reached within, nevertheless, to the light and he let it consume him. Like a dim opening at the end of a long tunnel, he focused on the light, and it grew until he believed in nothing else but the light and his perfect self at the center – strong, grounded and still. Stevie Vegas tapped into the magnificence of every human being, and of creation itself. In that moment, he was a perfect part of the Creator.

"It is you who has forsaken all hope, all grace and all love," Stevie said, between clenched teeth. "Did you honestly think that I would cower here like a child, in front of you – you who think nothing of turning a young boy away from the light, from every-thing that is good, and from those that love him? My brother Jem…and for that I loathe you and your kind."

The hooded figure rose in his seat, as if the air itself was supporting his weight. He moved closer to Stevie, but Stevie held his ground. The evilness spewed forth from the figure, and Stevie turned his face away.

"Umm, brave words," it hissed. "But I'm afraid they will not help you tonight, Stevie Vegas. Tonight you will find out your true destiny, and in that knowledge embrace your destiny. Let me see…were you aware, Stevie Vegas, that Jem is only your half-brother."

Stevie held firm, refusing to be drawn in by the hooded figure. "You lie, just a lie."

"It is no lie, Stevie Vegas. Have you ever wondered why Jem is drawn to the Shadowcasters, and tell me, have you ever wondered why Chris Barron was so intent on destroying your family? You mistakenly think he wants vengeance for what has been done to his son…but he has two sons, Stevie Vegas, and he is acting for both of them."

Stevie shook his head, unwilling to think any further.

"Yes, Stevie. You know now, don't you…know that Jem's father is Chris Barron."

Stevie slid down, losing sight of the light within. "No! No! It can't be true! Jem is no more Shadowcaster than I am."

The hooded figure moved closer still. So close, Stevie thought he would drown in those wild eyes. He was beginning to lose his resolve; the light was dimming and the darkness closing in. But before he spiraled further, he was almost knocked sideways by the force of a blinding, white light that was engulfing the cavern.

"Get away from him!" A huge voice thundered from behind. "You will not take my nephew into the black depths of your soul. His innocence is not to be bargained with."

Stevie turned slowly to see Aunt Bessie at the entrance to the antechamber. She was transformed, he thought, from a kindly, old aunt to a being of pulsating, absolute white light. Within her, he saw not just humanity, but righteousness too…and anger. Her arms were outstretched, her white hair flowing free and she was surrounded by the brightest and whitest of lights. Everything that is and ever was good seemed to be contained within the light and it was so brilliant he almost had to look away.

The Shadowcaster spun around to face her. "Ah, you come, old woman, or should I call you by your real name…Dharma the Light Bringer," he drawled. "Light will not find a way into my darkness, old woman," he hissed. "Your efforts are in vain. You will not save Jem; surely you know he is already a Greycaster. It will not be too long before he makes the transition to Shadowcaster and takes his rightful place in the Barron family…according to his bloodline. And you're precious young Stevie Vegas…"

Stevie felt the Shadowcaster's hand run across his cheek. It was a hand of death and he saw into that dark place where there was no return. He turned away from the chilling touch.

Aunt Bessie drew herself up to her full height and the pure whiteness of her aura expanded and surrounded them. Stevie could almost feel it cursing within his own veins. The blackness merged with the light and a spiral of colors whirled through the chasm, knocking him to the ground. "Get up…go," Aunt Bessie whispered. "I will be behind you. Go. Go now."

Stevie did not question her but turned and ran from the antechamber. As he moved quickly through the room, he paused quickly at Jacob Barron's bedside, but Jacob Barron was not there. The bed was empty. Stevie moved through the blackness steadily and it wasn't long before he reached Mary Lou, who was now being supported by Bren Lee.

"Quickly, there's no time to explain. We must run. Run, something is terribly wrong. We need to get out of here."

Bren Lee grabbed his arm. "Your Aunt Bessie. Stevie, we can't leave her."

Stevie shook him off, his face set with the determination that his aunt's actions to save him would not be in vain.

"Look, Aunt Bessie made it clear. She will catch us up. We must leave and leave now." He knew that if they didn't make their escape, they would all be caught in the Shadowcaster's lair. He sensed the balance of battle was being tested and Aunt Bessie would only hold out a few more minutes. He knew deep within his heart that their only option was to leave the blackness behind and only then would they be strong enough to fight.

With both of them supporting Mary Lou they made their way as quickly as they could out the door and through the terraced gardens to the woods. Behind them the sounds of the Barrons' social party continued unabated, as though nothing unnatural had ever occurred in the house.

They ran until they came to a clearing, where the tall trees formed a circle. They were breathing hard with the effort of running as fast as they could away from danger.

"Stop," Mary Lou said. "I need a second to get my breath."

Stevie nodded to Bren Lee. "Just one minute," he said. "No more."

Resting their hands on their knees, chests heaving, they rested. It was only a moment before danger was upon them. Stevie let out a huge yell, as several cloaked figures emerged from the darkness: Mary Lou's father, Chris Barron himself, Blake and Devlin Hood and Mr. Liechen. And another smaller figure, that of Jacob Barron. Their eyes locked and Stevie drove forward a blinding bolt of light from a place he did not know existed. It hit Jacob Barron and pushed him backward. In a split second, Chris Barron responded and a black force struck him in the stomach. He doubled over with pain, falling on his knees barely able to breathe.

"Stevie," Bren Lee said, jumping at the hooded group ready for combat.

The hooded Shadowcaster appeared then, from out of nowhere and with him was Jem who stood with the Shadowcasters.

"You see, Stevie Vegas, you are hopelessly outnumbered. And where is your Aunt Bessie now?" It let out a howling laugh – one that made Stevie's veins run hot with rage and injustice – if this thing had harmed Aunt Bessie..."

"They are indeed most helplessly outnumbered – including your mother," Chris Barron said, beckoning to the valet who had Stevie's mother in an arm lock. "Take her. She has made it clear to me that she will never join us, but Jem...our son...well that's a different story."

Stevie's mother stumbled towards them, and they backed up against each other: Mary Lou, Stevie, Bren Lee and Sylvia...but they were hopelessly surrounded and hopelessly outnumbered.

Stevie searched desperately for Aunt Bessie, and projected his thoughts outward. If ever they needed a miracle, it was now. He concentrated on her image and focused, as if trying to summon her to the clearing.

Far off, he heard the sounds of thunder and noticed the wind rising, so that the leaves in the trees rustled and branches swayed. And then he knew. Aunt Bessie was coming all right and so was a very dangerous storm.

Chapter 22

An Almighty Force

The wind picked up, lifting the coats of the Shadowcasters and blowing branches and leaves across the clearing. Stevie and his mum looked at one other and nodded. This was the moment they had prepared for. In a split second, Bren Lee reached into his pocket and pushed the ancient amulet into Sylvia's hands. She nodded, understanding what he'd given her.

Stevie projected his thoughts into his mother's mind, while the wind became a maelstrom around them.

"Mum…are you all right…Jem, what can we do?"

"We are not leaving here without him, Stevie. Never."

He saw the fear in her eyes…but something else too…determination. He knew that whatever happened, he had to get Jem away from the Shadowcasters…before they turned him completely. He threw out his thoughts to his younger brother.

"Jem," he whispered in his thought mind. "I'm not letting you go. Jem, can you hear me?"

He looked across the clearing, and locked eyes with his brother, driving his thoughts even harder into the recesses of Jem's mind.

"Jem, can you hear me? We are brothers and I will not leave you. I don't care what you've done, or thought, or want to be. You need only know one thing and that is you are, and always will be, my brother."

For a long moment, Jem didn't make contact, and just as Stevie was about to give up, he heard the faintest thoughts penetrating his mind. "Yes, Stevie, I can hear you thanks to the training the Hoods…and my father are beginning to give me."

Stevie pushed back. "Jem, you might feel like they are giving you power but it can only end in your destruction. You are not a

Shadowcaster and never will be. My father…your father, Alexander Vegas, loves you. I don't care what Chris Barron has told you. Despite the past, you are a Vegas and half Illuminator. Don't turn your back on us, Jem. Don't turn away from the light."

Jem sneered, bitterness rising from the depths of his being. "You think you can tell me what to do, Stevie. Like you have been doing all my life. Do you honestly think I want to stay with you and become an Illuminator? You know nothing, Stevie, nothing. Illuminators have no power or influence – you are like blades of grass bending in a strong wind. Shadowcasters, on the other hand, command everything. You, Stevie, are on the losing side and it's not too late to join us. They want you too, not just me."

It was Stevie's turn to sneer. "I will no more join the Shadowcasters than use my powers for my own gain. Don't you understand, Jem; it comes down to the choices we make. Don't make the wrong choice now. You'll regret it. Think of Mum, if you can't think of our dad."

Jem smiled into the darkness and kept his gaze locked on Stevie. "It was you who always had Mum's attention. You and you're stupid skateboarding and always having to be the best…the hero in the story. Well I'm writing my own story now."

With that, Stevie felt a blinding pain in his head and the hooded Shadowcaster stepped forward.

Through the pain, Stevie felt Bren Lee's gentle guidance and he remembered his training and the discipline he had learned at Bren Lee's side. "Still you mind," Bren Lee whispered.

"Yes, Stevie, don't let their thoughts in," Mary Lou urged.

And then his mother. "You will not take my boys away from me." She let go of their hands and stepped forward, toward the hooded Shadowcasters, a mother's love at that moment, the most powerful force on the earth. The amulet in her hand glowed white-hot and began radiating power.

As she stepped forward the wind began to lift even more, and

DAWN OF THE SHADOWCASTERS

the rain began to fall. Not gentle rain, but hard, blistering rain that hurt at its touch. Lightening crackled in the sky and Stevie wondered if this was, indeed, Aunt Bessie's power. He searched his thoughts for her and in the dim recesses of his mind, he found her.

"The power of three, Stevie, the unbreakable circle. Join with me and your mother, like we have rehearsed so many times before. The power of three, at its best, is the strongest of all."

At that moment, Bren Lee took a large, pulsating crystal from his coat pocket – an ancient Illuminator stone. He pushed it into Stevie's hands and it was hot to the touch. In a split second Aunt Bessie appeared within the circle and Stevie threw her the stone. Stevie's own stone began to throb with a power he could feel coming from somewhere deep within him. They were three now, three Illuminators and their power stones.

He 'heard' his mother's voice. "Yes, Aunt Bessie, Stevie…now, before it's too late."

In an instant Chris Barron stepped forward, bracing himself against the wind which was howling around the group – Illuminator and Shadowcaster alike. But it was too late.

Aunt Bessie, Stevie and Sylvia had already merged their Illuminator powers and the powers of the three Illuminator stones, and a great white shard of light shot out from them, skywards. In an instant Aunt Bessie had lifted her voice to the night sky and uttered the words Stevie did not know, but was familiar nevertheless. "*Nosce te ipsum*, 'Know thyself!'"

At first there was stillness. The wind dropped and the Shadowcasters looked at the Illuminators not really knowing what to do. And then it began happening. Everyone in the circle – Shadowcaster and Illuminator saw themselves clearly as if a mirror had been placed before them. The Shadowcasters not only saw themselves in all their evil, but felt the pain and suffering they had caused others. Similarly, Stevie, Bren Lee and the Illuminators felt the power of rightness flowing through their veins. If there were a balance of good and evil, in that one split second, the balance fell on the side of Illuminators. This was a moment that was known in Illuminator history as 'Luminous,' the power of absolute truth.

Taking advantage of the Shadowcaster's confusion, Sylvia ran forward to get Jem, but it was too late, the Shadowcasters had turned and were running back to the Barron estate. Only the hooded Shadowcaster remained, doubled over at first. But as the wind died and rain eased, he drew himself up.

"Old woman, you think you can beat me with your silly parlor games. Do you think I care about the pain and suffering I cause. No, I relish it. It gives me power. I gloat, I laugh, I enjoy it all, every last bit of suffering I feel coursing through my veins and piercing my heart."

His yellow eyes flashed without mercy, as he raised his hand toward Aunt Bessie…

"No…NO…NO!" Stevie yelled, as the flame was released from the Shadowcasters hand, and travelled towards his aunt. It hit her, and in a millisecond, she vanished into the smoky air."

Stevie stepped forward toward the hooded Shadowcaster and summoning the rage and the hatred and hurt he felt for all the Shadowcasters he let the light within him build until it was the hot, white light of justice. He took that unforgiving, all judging light, which was emanating from the depths of his soul, and projected it towards the hooded Shadowcaster. It hit him in the heart and, like Aunt Bessie, the Shadowcaster disappeared into the smoky air. His wild, yellow eyes were the last thing Stevie Vegas saw before he collapsed, spent, into his mother's arms. He let the darkness come then. Blessed, merciful darkness where he did not have to think about Jem, about Aunt Bessie and, most importantly, about what the future held.

As the last of the wind died and the rain stopped, the small group stood in the clearing alone. Sylvia Vegas cradled her son in her lap and Bren Lee comforted her. Only Mary Lou stood apart. She gazed into the blackness that was the night sky. Deep within her, in a far off place, she felt the seed of the Shadowcaster grow…but something else too. A light, Aunt Bessie's light began to move within her. It surrounded the black seed of the Shadowcaster within her, covering it and extinguishing it until it was no more. Mary Lou was now an Illuminator. She touched Stevie's forehead with her hand, and her hand was warm to the touch.

"Stevie, come back, wake up." He heard her voice, which penetrated his blackness and despair.

As he opened his eyes, he saw her face, bright with tears and illuminated by the stars, which were no longer shrouded by the dark, storm clouds. He looked at her then, seeing the face of hope that would sustain them all in the coming months.

Epilogue

The Vegas family left Valley Dale in the spring. They had no choice but to pack up and leave. They were long days and even longer nights. Almost overnight Sylvia and Alexander's vet practice dried up. Doors slammed in their faces for no other reason than Chris Barron wielded an almighty power…everywhere.

They had fought to get Jem back, but even the police were not interested in helping them. It was as if the whole town had turned against them. They tried hiring a lawyer and going through the courts, but Chris Barron provided DNA proof that he was Jem's father, and continued to smear the Vegas name, saying Sylvia was unstable and Stevie was no better. It was no environment for a young 12-year-old, he said and father and son should spend time together. Stevie supposed he had used a combination of money, mind games and manipulation to get what he wanted. Without money to keep fighting the case, the Vegas family conceded defeat…for the time being.

And Aunt Bessie, there was an empty void in their hearts that nothing could fill. Bren Lee's family tried at first to find her, but as the months wore on and there was no sign of her – as if she had disappeared into thin air – they gave up, beaten and without hope.

In those long months, acceptance and resignation were so much a part of their souls. Only Mary Lou who had come to live with them, despite the threats from her father, had any sort of hope for the future. She was the hope in their lives, when there was no respite from defeat and disappointment.

And so beaten down by mounting bills, and an unpaid mortgage, they had given in to Alexander's brother's suggestion they move inland for a couple of months, across the vast stretch of land that lay to the east, to the mountain country. It was almost on the other side of the country, but the Vegas family figured they had no choice. White Cap Mountain, the home of his father's parents' farm, was to become their new home in the months ahead.

Stevie held his mum's hand tightly as they left Valley Dale. These days, she did nothing but cry and his heart ached for her. He missed Jem too, so much so that for a time he stopped skating, stopped going to school and stopped seeing anyone but Bren Lee. All he wanted to do was stare into the darkness and the growing bitterness that was his life now.

But he held tight to his parents…and to Mary Lou. He knew somehow they would get through it, together. He also knew that despite Jem turning away from the light, his brother would one day return to him. In this he had a resolute faith.

Faith, hope, and a stubborn determination to put one foot in front of the other and keep going, got Stevie and his family through those early months, when it seemed the whole world had turned against them.

But the family knew they had no choice but to move to White Cap Mountain farm – it was all they could do. And so, Stevie held his mum's hand and smiled faintly at Mary Lou and his father in turn, as the car left Valley Dale behind. They took along Jem's dog Fluffy who had been pining for Jem, but every time Stevie looked at him it reminded him of Jem. All he could do for the miserable dog was let his dad look after him. There was no love left in his heart for something that belonged to the brother he'd lost; the brother who was turning into a Shadowcaster for all he knew.

The journey was long and hard and somehow the more miles they put between themselves and Valley Dale…and Jem, the harder it got. Stevie watched the countryside slip away through the thick lens of the car's window, as one state after another passed by. He had lost count of the cheap motel rooms they stayed in, but all roads end somewhere and eventually White Cap Mountain came into view. There was still the aftermath of a winter's snow on the mountain's peaks, but below green wooded hills gave way to farmland pastures.

Stevie had been told that White Cap Mountain Farm was located near Aurora Falls, a small skiing village in winter and a service town for the surrounding farms in the off-season. As they approached the small town en route to the farm, Stevie caught his breath and, for the first time, really looked at the scene unfolding through his window. It wasn't so much what he saw, as what he heard.

Voices grew louder in his mind, as he approached the town. He looked suspiciously at Mary Lou.

"Did you hear that?" he whispered, not wanting to disturb his mum and dad in the front of the car.

Mary Lou's eyes were wide. "Hear it – you betcha," she said, the excitement evident in her eyes. "It's the voices of Illuminators, Stevie. I know them, I can hear their welcome."

Stevie smiled for the first time since that night in the clearing, when they had lost Jem and Aunt Bessie.

"I hear it too, Mary Lou," he said. "It's like the sound of a running river – there are people within this town who are Illuminators."

"But how? Why?" Mary Lou whispered.

Stevie looked out the window, at the timbered homes, and the people on the street. They seemed ordinary, nothing magical about them…but still there were the voices, welcoming them, and something else – a voice above the others, as if coming from the mountain itself.

"Don't doubt why you are here, Stevie Vegas. You are precisely where you should be, at exactly the right time. Trust us, trust me."

Mary Lou heard the words too.

"Stevie, who are they, and who does that voice belong too? These people look ordinary – like you and me. Whoever it is knows how to read minds. Should we trust them?"

Stevie shook his head. "Trust. No, Mary Lou. We trust no one and nothing but each other. Right."

She nodded. "Yes Stevie. No one."

He looked back through the window again. They had left the town behind and were snaking their way up the mountain to the farm. The voices in his head grew dim. Once he had trusted his ability to read minds, and his Illuminator powers but in the end, he had lost a great deal and he was not prepared to lose again, or trust again. His resolve hardened and he sat back letting the outside view recede for a moment.

"Wherever you are, Aunt Bessie, know that you are needed," he thought. "Needed to fight the oncoming war with the Shadowcasters, because I am not giving up on my brother. Whatever it takes, I will walk away with him at my side next time."

Mary Lou reached for his hand and he gave her a half-hearted smile. He'd forgotten she was one of them and could read his mind. At that moment the sun burst from behind a cloud, illuminating the car. Had Aunt Bessie been with them, she would have said it was an omen of good things to come.

**LODESTONE
BOOKS**

Lodestone Books is a new imprint, which offers a broad spectrum of subjects in YA/NA literature. Compelling reading, the Teen/Young/New Adult reader is sure to find something edgy, enticing and innovative. From dystopian societies, through a whole range of fantasy, horror, science fiction and paranormal fiction, all the way to the other end of the sphere, historical drama, steam-punk adventure, and everything in between. You'll find stories of crime, coming of age and contemporary romance. Whatever your preference you will discover it here.